PASSIONATE CONCERTO

PASSIONATE CONCERTO

REBECCA BENJAMIN

ROBERT HALE · LONDON

© Rebecca Benjamin 1993
First published in Great Britain 1993

ISBN 0 7090 4922 6

Robert Hale Limited
Clerkenwell House
Clerkenwell Green
London EC1R 0HT

Printed and bound by Interpint Ltd.,
Valletta, Malta.

One

Natasha snatched her hands abruptly from the piano keys as if she had been stung. She lifted her enquiring eyes to the cause of the swift halt to her opening chords, the sharp tapping of a baton on the wooden music stand. For only a moment she met the glare aimed at her from the maestro's steely eyes before lowering her own dark eyes to the fingers which lay clenched in her lap. Tears of indignation pricked in the back of those eyes, but she bit her lower lip hard, determined not to let him get the better of her. She must not give in, show any weakness. She must prove herself despite his antagonism towards her since the first rehearsal.

'I don't know what it is,' she had confided to her close friend and agent, Suzy Dannovitch, after an exhausting day at the end of the previous week, 'but he seems to have a grudge against me.'

'Rubbish, Tash, you're tired. Anyone would be in this heat. Go home, shower and change and I'll call for you at eight. We'll find that quiet little pub down by the river and you can relax and forget him.'

It had been hard for Natasha to do either of these last two things. She had to admit she was the most nervous she had ever been in her life about Tuesday's concert in the Royal Albert Hall. It was her first ever prom. She had been a regular promenader since her early teens and her dream had always been to be up

5

on that stage with a world-famous conductor and a top-ranking orchestra and now that dream was coming true.

'I arranged this concert because I have every confidence in your genius,' Suzy had assured her later that night as the cool breeze from the river at last gave them respite from a scorching summer's day. 'You've made it, my girl. Believe in yourself. Give yourself a break.'

'I was fine until today. My practising has been going well and Piers is wonderful with his advice. I really feel my technique improves each session I've had with him.'

'So why let a tiny little thing get to you?'

Natasha laughed.

'You could hardly call Anton Martineau tiny or little! He intimidates me, physically as well as mentally.'

'Well, don't let him. You're as good a musician as him, any day.'

Suzy's words of advice returned to her as she prepared to rehearse the concerto again. She equalled the conductor's gaze as he stood, his baton poised, the orchestra on their marks. Determination oozing out of every pore, she performed the first movement brilliantly.

'OK, everybody. That was much better. We'll have a break then straight through the whole work. Back here at eleven on the dot.'

Anton Martineau stepped down from the rostrum and left the stage. Natasha gazed round the massive arena, empty now, trying to imagine the hundreds of enthusiastic people, young and old, who would be there that night. A thrill of excitement passed through her. She must keep her spirits up at all costs then she knew she would do well.

She stood up, suddenly aware that the entire orchestra had sat there patiently waiting for her to move from her seat. As she left the stage, one of the first violinists caught up with her.

'He's gorgeous, that man,' she sighed. 'We all love him. The orchestra plays so well under his baton.'

Natasha smiled politely, unconvinced.

Why did everybody say the same of him? What was it that made everyone think that the sun shone out of his...?

She stopped the indecent thoughts that flooded into her head with a giggle, descending the steep flight of steps that led to the artists' dressing-rooms. Entering the door that said 'Soloist' she poured herself a cup of coffee and sank on the sofa.

What was so special about him anyway? she still wondered. To her, he seemed no more than a self-opinionated male who enjoyed a powerful position over so many people.

A rap on her door brought her down to earth.

'Come in.'

The towering form that stood framed in the doorway almost succeeded in daunting her.

'I said, "Come in",' she managed to repeat, pulling her confidence up from somewhere near the floor. 'Sit down. Coffee?'

He shook his head, but sat opposite Natasha on an upright chair, giving him a dominant position over her.

'I'll come straight to the point,' he began without a flicker of expression in his deep-set blue eyes.

She studied the firm line of his jaw, his golden hair

curling into the nape of his neck, waiting.

'The Tchaikovsky number one,' he went on, 'is notorious for being a powerhouse of a piece, for all of us, but especially for the soloist.'

'Yes?'

'When I agreed to do this performance I was led to believe it would be with Lill or Ashkenazy or ... or another top-class male pianist. It needs strength and stamina which, quite frankly Miss Spitzen, I doubt you possess.'

Natasha leapt to her feet, in a moment of anger, her fist clenched. Quick as a flash, he grabbed her wrist tightly in front of him. Reaching down, he took hold of her other wrist no less firmly and brought both hands up before her reddened face.

'Mind your precious fingers, Miss Spitfire. You don't want to ruin your livelihood, do you? Save all your energy for the Tchaikovsky. I tell you, you're going to need it.'

'Don't you worry, Mr Marvellous. I can promise you, my performance will equal, no, better, any male you might mention and your musical reputation will remain unscathed.'

She wrenched her hands from his grasp and stood before him, her breasts heaving with the exertion. Aware of his eyes travelling swiftly over her slim body, she pulled her fingers through her long black hair and tossed her head defiantly. Without another word she crossed the room and held open the door.

'I would like to drink my coffee now and be allowed ten minutes' peace and quiet. Eleven o'clock on the dot, I believe you requested.' She spoke in her sweetest voice. 'Then we'll see what a mere slip of a girl can do!'

'How did your final rehearsal go, darling?'

'Oh, Piers. It's you.'

'Of course it's me. Well, answer me, how did it go?'

Natasha sighed, a far-away look in her eyes.

'Are you all right, Tash? It did go well, didn't it?'

'It's a long story, but yes it was fine.'

She spoke so quietly Piers had to ask her to repeat her answer.

'You'd better begin at the beginning.'

Natasha spoke at length of her battle with Anton Martineau.

'But he's such a sweet man, by all accounts.'

'Huh!'

'And the concerto?'

The next ten minutes were filled with Natasha's detailed description of her performance in the final rehearsal, each phrase of music, each chord, each intricate passage that demanded her utmost skill and concentration.

'Great, my love,' Piers managed to say as Natasha paused for breath, 'but what did the maestro think?'

'He was full of praise for the orchestra, picking out the instrumentalists he felt had excelled themselves, psyching them up for tonight.'

'And you?'

'Oh, me? He stepped down off his pedestal, came round the piano to me and stage-whispered, "Not bad for a slip of a girl", and laughed, right in front of everyone, and they, like so many creeps, laughed too. What a way to treat someone, Piers, after I'd played so well. But don't you worry, I'm not going to be browbeaten by the likes of Mr Marvellous. Just let him wait till tonight. He'll never again experience such a brilliant performance. I'll show him!'

'That's my Tasha! Now get some sleep for a couple of hours. I know you'll play better than ever before and I'll be with you in every note. See you afterwards.'

Half an hour and another phone call to Suzy later, Natasha hoped she was almost purged of Anton Martineau's superiority. It was time for her to accept Piers's advice and take the obligatory pre-concert nap. She ate a light lunch with a cup of herb tea, stripped down to her robe and went to lie on her bed. Somehow, however, sleep eluded her. Every time she closed her eyes, a face loomed before her, a strong, lean face framed in deep gold, whose stern blue eyes penetrated her mind.

'Go away, you horrid man,' she said aloud, turning to her other side as if turning from him.

She tried lying on her back, her front, her sides. She attempted reading, but on this occasion it had no soporific effect. She listened to her favourite Beatles tape, but to no avail. She simply could not sleep.

By the time Suzy arrived to accompany her to the Albert Hall she was feeling anything but calm and collected in readiness for her exacting role.

'It's that man again,' she scowled.

'I thought I'd succeeded in putting him in perspective in your mind.'

'The trouble is he kept recurring. I feel like a wet rag. How on earth am I going to carry out my promise, or was it a threat, to him and prove that I can play?'

'I repeat, you've got to get things in perspective. The important people tonight are the audience. Think of all those men and women who will come to hear a terrific piece of music played by an up-and-coming, new, young pianist. Those young promenaders will relate to you. It will be your job to lift them out of the ordinary into something extraordinary. You can do it for them, you know you can. And if it helps at all, you can do it to spite him.'

'What would I do without you, Suzy?' laughed Natasha, giving her friend an enormous bear hug.

'Starve, I shouldn't wonder!'

By now Natasha had showered and was standing in her skimpy underwear.

'Help me into this.'

She stepped into the deep turquoise dress, which suited her dark complexion and almost jet black hair. Fitted in the bodice and down past her hips, the dress flared out gently towards the ground. It flattered her slim curvaceous body.

'You'll stun them before you start!' exclaimed Suzy. 'It'll be a bonus to hear you play!'

The taxi whisked them through the busy London streets round to the artists' entrance at the rear of the Albert Hall.

'Evening, Miss,' smiled the porter as he let her pass through, with Suzy close on her heels.

Carefully, she descended the steep steps and entered her dressing-room, noticing the tray of drinks on the table.

'Do you want anything?'

'I feel as if I could do with one, but I'd better stick to Perrier, please. I need all my wits about me.'

'You don't mind if I have a whisky, do you? I can drink for the two of us.'

Suzy gulped back her first drink and poured herself a second.

'Go easy. I can't have my agent being drunk and disorderly in charge of a pianist!'

She opened the two envelopes that were lying on

the table. One was from her brother, Tom, who was in Canada, wishing her luck. The other was from her mother.

You know I'm thinking of you, it said. *I'm with you in spirit and I shall be glued to the radio.*

It would have been lovely if her mother could have made the journey up from the West Country, but her failing health made thoughts of that impossible.

A bell could be heard ringing somewhere in the hall.

'Five minutes to the overture.'

Natasha nodded. Suddenly, she felt sick, as if a thousand butterflies had just hatched out of their chrysalides inside her stomach.

'Perhaps I will have just a small one.'

Then Suzy had gone, following the members of the orchestra up the stairs, she to her seat in the stalls, the musicians to the stage. Natasha heard a familiar voice outside her door as the maestro himself made his way to the great hall. She sipped the tiny amount of whisky she had allowed herself and began to feel slightly calmer, hearing the roar from the audience as Anton Martineau appeared on the rostrum. She sank back into the sofa when she had finished her drink, and inhaled deep, relaxing gulps of air.

This was her big moment, the moment she had longed for, her first appearance at a Henry Wood Promenade Concert, and she hoped not her last. She heard another distant roar as the overture ended.

'Miss Spitzen,' said a voice outside the door.

'OK, thank you.'

She felt composed as she opened the door and climbed the stairs in readiness. She still had some minutes to wait as the applause continued. Anton Martineau brushed past her without even noticing her on his return from his second curtain call, then the audience grew quiet and extra orchestra members joined the rest on the stage. She had expected a delay as the piano had to be placed correctly, but she wished she had not left her room quite so immediately.

'Heave – ho!' came the shout from the exciteable promenaders and she smiled at the memory of shouting the very same thing, as tradition has it, at the lifting of the piano lid.

'All set?' whispered a voice behind her and she turned smartly to catch an almost approving glance from the conductor.

She nodded, finding herself looking away from such penetrating eyes.

Come on, Tasha, she cajoled herself. No male such as this is going to upstage you.

Swiftly, she was transported into the bright lights, partly by her own adrenalin that began to flow, partly on the strength of the maestro as his hand lifted her arm, propelling her before him. She felt the warmth of the reception as she stood facing the crowds, who were no longer figments of her imagination. Her apprehension slowly ebbed away as she sat and made herself comfortable at the piano.

Anton Martineau faced his orchestra, baton poised. The audience obediently became hushed. He stole a glance at Natasha with an expression that she did not fully understand. But there was no time to deliberate on that as the orchestra's opening bars of Tchaikovsky's First Piano Concerto gave her her cue.

Gradually, as she became more and more engrossed in her playing, any remaining nervousness left her and she became immersed completely in the music. She felt power in her forearms and magic in her fingers as she leapt from one demanding passage to another. Frequently, piano and orchestra blending together, she caught Anton Martineau's eye as she took the tempo from his baton, but their discord of the morning was forgotten as she was aware of carrying out Suzy's forecast of lifting everyone into the extra-ordinary.

After the exhilarating finale to the first movement, the orchestra took a little time to retune their instruments, giving Natasha an opportunity to compose herself for the gentle contrast of the second. She avoided looking up at the conductor, knowing his eyes searched for hers. It was not until they were ready to begin that she raised her dark eyes and nodded almost imperceptibly. Again, she failed to understand his message, but she at least registered approval.

Was she winning? she wondered as she became involved once more in the music, feeling the emotion of the slow movement through the rapt silence of the large audience.

The eruption of sound from the listeners after the piano and orchestra together sped to the climax underlined their success.

'Bravo!' and 'Encore!' resounded round the hall as Natasha stood, one hand on the piano to steady her dizzy head, to take her bow. She stepped back to shake the conductor's hand and he bent ostentatiously to kiss hers. Then holding her hand in a vice-like grip that she could not release, they stood side by side to acknowledge the applause.

She returned to the arena four times, twice on her own, before the stamping and cheering began to die down and at last she found herself floating down the steps to her room. Almost immediately, Suzy was with her, hugging the breath out of her, followed closely by Piers, who did the same. She soon found herself surrounded by a surge of well-wishers, auto-graph hunters and photographers.

She heard words like, 'Wonderful!' and 'Unique!' 'Out of this world!', 'Best ever!', 'Genius!' and 'Perfect!'.

Despite her euphoria and the novelty of signing autographs, she was relieved when her newly-found fans dispersed to the second half of the concert which was about to begin and only her two close friends remained.

'What did the great man think?'

'Who knows. He has said nothing.'

'You realize why that is, don't you? He doesn't like to admit he was wrong. He's not used to stooping that low!'

'Suzy, don't bitch,' laughed Piers as the telephone rang.

'Mummy!' exclaimed Natasha, waving to her com-panions to be quiet. 'Yes, I am ... Thank you ... Yes, yes, I promise ... OK, see you soon. Bye.'

The next morning, Natasha woke with a mixture of emotions revolving in her head. She felt buoyant with her success, yet somehow flat. She bounced with energy, but did not know what to do. In the midst of her achievement, there was something missing.

At 9.30, Suzy breezed in with an armful of daily papers.

'Rave reviews!' she grinned, throwing her load down on the table. 'Take a look.'

'I daren't. You read one to me, will you?'

For the next half an hour they read one review after

another and all the papers agreed on the brilliance of
Natasha's performance the previous evening.

'Don't let this go to your head, though, Tash. This is
only a beginning.'

Natasha nodded pensively.

'What is it?'

'It just seems strange, that's all.'

'What?'

'Not a word from Mr Marvellous.'

'No. Still, forget him. With a bit of luck you won't
have the pleasure of playing under his baton again. I
must be off. Got a busy schedule today. Bye!'

No sooner had Suzy let herself out of the front door
when the doorbell rang.

'What's she forgotten, I wonder,' Natasha murmured as she went to open it, then, 'Oh!' she gasped at
the huge bouquet of flowers that hid the delivery lady
on the step.

'Miss Spitzen?'

'Yes. Thank you,' she added as the bouquet descended into her outstretched arms.

She managed to close the door and stagger into the
kitchen, putting the flowers down on the work-top to
search for a message. She ripped open the tiny envelope and read, simply, *Wonderful!*

So he had approved of her performance after all,
and more importantly, had allowed himself to admit
it.

After arranging the flower in two crystal vases, her
recuperation was complete. This was just the tonic
she had needed to recharge her enthusiasm and she
knew all along what she should be doing. She had an
important piano recital coming up in ten days' time,
in the Wigmore Hall no less, and her success there

could influence the recording contract Suzy was trying to negotiate. So practice, practice, practice had to
be her single-minded occupation until then.

Smiling to herself at winning the great man's approval, she devoted the next few hours to perfecting
the pieces she and Piers had chosen for the recital.
Her love of the piano had begun when, as a young girl,
she had sat on the long piano stool next to her
grandmother, watching the nimble fingers chase each
other up and down the black and white notes. It had
been the same dear old lady who had supported and
encouraged her as she passed one exam after another
and won the scholarship to the Paris Conservatoire.

Piers had entered the scene much later, when she
began making a name for herself in provincial concert
halls. As she approached his flat that afternoon she
still retained the eagerness injected by the arrival of
the bouquet.

'That proves I won, doesn't it, Piers?' she laughed.
'But trust him not to sign his name. That would be
expecting too much!'

Piers shared her amusement, and kissed her affectionately, but said nothing. They walked together into
his music room.

'How's the practising going?'

Throughout the week Natasha glanced many times at
her flowers, taking in their scent which gradually
faded as the petals withered. She spent some time
making what she hoped was the beginning of a very
thick scrapbook from the newspaper reviews and a
short article in the *Radio Times* about her successful
debut at the Proms. She felt it was too vain to be doing
it for herself, but planned to give it to her mother

when she had filled it. It would compensate for her inability to be present at her daughter's concerts. Natasha decided she would include parts of the Prom programme which Suzy had given her on Tuesday night.

Turning the pages slowly, she cut out the heading page which named the orchestra, conductor, soloist, and the pieces that were to be played. Then she found the photograph of herself, taken at a tiny studio in St John's Wood. It was quite a flattering photo, she thought, showing her full lips and straight nose beneath warm dark eyes and a cascade of black wavy hair. She cut this out, with the passage of information about her career so far.

From the opposite page, Anton Martineau's portrait caused a surge of warmth to flood through her. The fact that a photograph could have such an effect on her was disconcerting, to say the least, but she excused her body's reaction with the presence of the flowers on the table before her. She studied the face for a moment.

Yes, it was probably what people would describe as handsome, a strong face with determination in the jaw-line as well as in that inscrutable aloof expression in the eyes. She had witnessed that at first hand. She would love to know what was going on in that deep-blond head of his.

No, she wouldn't. She stopped her reverie abruptly. What was she thinking of, letting her mind wander like this?

She turned back to the job in hand, carefully working the scissors around the photograph and its accompanying information.

'*Anton Martineau, aged 32, studied at the Royal*

College of Music and St John's College, Oxford...
There followed more details of his musical education
and background. *He has conducted in America,
Canada, the Far East and many European venues.
This is the third year he has performed at the Prom-
enade Concerts....*

Why am I taking such an interest in his life and
career? Natasha repeatedly asked herself as she stuck
all the cuttings in the scrapbook. He means absolutely
nothing to me. I'm just glad to have proved him wrong,
that's all.

The day of her recital dawned hot and humid. The
temperature in London at midnight had been as
warm as an average summer's day, and Natasha's
sleep had been intermittent, full of strange imaginings,
half-way between awake and asleep.

In one, she was lost in a field of beautiful flowers,
dotted with tiny envelopes which opened and spoke in
a deep masculine voice saying, 'Wonderful', over and
over again.

In another, Anton Martineau's face had loomed up
through the piano, his piercing blue eyes inscrutable
as ever.

Natasha crawled lazily out of bed in answer to the
telephone. It was Suzy, as expected.

'All set for tonight?'

'Yep.'

'You sound a bit dozy this morning.'

'That's because I had a bad night in this heat.'

'Well, I've got some news that might wake you up
somewhat. I've had an unbelievably hectic few days,
mainly on your behalf, I might add. How do you fancy
playing in Canada?'

Natasha gasped. 'When?'

'In the spring. I'll give you the details later.'

'Great. I'll have to let Tom know.'

'More work, too. You certainly set everyone alight the other night, you know. They're all queuing up for your services.'

'Brilliant! Thanks Suzy and well done.'

'It's you that's well done, my girl. Oh, by the way, I saw a friend of yours the other evening, in that little Italian restaurant in Chelsea.'

'Who?'

'The great man himself, looking as devastating as ever. He was alone and if I hadn't been trying to impress a client, I'd have been tempted to join him.'

'Did he speak to you?'

'Are you joking? No, he merely acknowledged me with a nod. He's a cool one, to be sure.'

Natasha's recital went well. The hall was almost full with an appreciative audience, including the representative of the record company who joined her and Suzy and Piers in her dressing-room afterwards. As on the previous occasion, they had to appease the autograph hunters before turning to business.

'Congratulations, Miss Spitzen, both on a magnificent performance this evening and on the recording contract which my company would be delighted to confirm. I have provisionally arranged with Ms Dannovitch that you attend tomorrow at 10 a.m. to sign contracts. Is that possible?'

'It certainly is, and thank you. I'll be there in the morning.'

Suzy accompanied him out of the room leaving Natasha alone with her teacher. Piers simply wrapped his arms warmly round her and she nestled her head on his shoulder.

'My prodigy,' he beamed, kissing her on the nose and she responded by putting her arms around his neck and squeezing him tightly.

The door opened quietly behind Piers and Natasha froze as, over his shoulder she found herself face to face with Anton Martineau. She dropped her arms immediately, but it was too late.

'Sorry. I didn't know.' He coughed, backing out.

Piers turned at the sound of the voice and released Natasha.

She dashed to the closing door, following the conductor out along the corridor.

'Mr Martineau,' she called.

He swung round, an impatient expression on his face.

'Call me Anton, for heaven's sake.'

'Piers is only my piano tutor.'

It sounded so limp, as though she were making excuses for herself. That was the last impression she wanted to give. She stopped, suddenly wondering why Anton Martineau was there. Had he been listening to her recital? she wondered. It was a good job she had not seen him in the audience.

'I just came to say I enjoyed your playing, that's all,' he said rather ungraciously. 'I came out of curiosity.'

'Curiosity? Charming!'

'I wanted to answer a question that's been at the back of my mind. Was your playing of the Tchaikovsky at the Proms a fluke, or are you really showing promise of being a great pianist?'

Cheek! she thought, feeling the anger flare up in her face.

'And what's your verdict, then?'

'I think the appropriate judgement must be, "Not bad for a slip of a girl", don't you?'

Sparks flashed in her eyes as she stood glaring up at him.

'I don't know why you bothered.'

'Sorry!' he laughed. 'It's worth saying that just to see you mad. Actually, I'm now convinced it wasn't a fluke.'

Well, that was a back-handed compliment, if ever she heard one. He was walking away from her now.

'We'll meet again, no doubt,' he said as he reached the corner.

'Oh, Mr Martineau, er, Anton,' she called.

He raised his eyebrows quizzically.

'Thanks for the flowers.'

'Flowers? What are you talking about?'

'The flowers I received after the Prom – they were from you, weren't they?'

'My dear girl, what put that ridiculous idea into your head?'

'I thought....'

'Thought? You didn't think at all. Come down to earth, will you? As if I'd dream of....'

Two

Natasha did not wait to hear the rest of the sentence, having fled to the safety of her room. She slammed the door behind her, leaning heavily on it as if to keep him out. She was flushed and breathing quickly, unaware of Piers who stood in exactly the same spot as she had left him.

'What ever is the matter?'

Natasha jumped, then tried to regain her composure.

'Oh, nothing, really. It's my fault entirely. I've just made an absolute fool of myself to Anton Martineau. You know the flowers I assumed were from him?'

'Yes.'

'Well, they weren't, that's all.'

'I know!'

'What? Why didn't you tell me?' she shouted, angrily. 'You let me assume he sent them. You didn't put me right when I told you about them, did you? Do you know who did send them, then?'

'Yes.'

'Who?'

'Actually, it was me.'

Struck dumb by the bolt that had hit her, Natasha sat down and put her head in her hands.

'Oh!' was all she could manage to say. After a few moments, she looked up at her teacher who had not taken his eyes from her face all this time.

'Thanks. You shouldn't have,' she said, not liking his expression.

Suddenly, he knelt before her, taking her hand in his.

'I felt there was no easier way to say what I think of you – Wonderful – I believed you would guess the bouquet was from me and was hurt at your delight when he was assumed to be the sender. That's why I said nothing.'

Natasha swallowed hard. Was she hearing correctly? Was this man of whom she was very fond, but in whom she saw no physical attraction whatsoever, trying to declare his love for her?

'I'm very grateful, Piers,' she began carefully, 'and I look upon you as a friend and support.'

The more she deliberated on it the more she rejected any other form of relationship with Piers. She had always found him rather effeminate and affected. She had even wondered if he had homosexual tendencies. She flinched as he leaned nearer to her in a clumsy attempt to kiss her. He sat back, recovering some of his composure.

'I have grown extremely fond of you, Tasha, my love.'

'And I of you, Piers. You know that, but only as a brother.'

'Perhaps now you know of my feelings you could grow to think differently of me?'

'Piers. Can we drop this, please? It's late and I'm tired. I need to be alone to sort out my addled brain.'

'I understand, my pet. Can I order a taxi for you?'

She nodded. Please go, she said silently, closing her eyes while he phoned for her cab.

'In ten minutes outside the artists' entrance. OK?'

'Thanks. I'll see you next week, usual time at my lesson. Goodnight, Piers.'

When he had closed the door from the outside, she collected her belongings and made her way quietly along the corridor to the exit. True to his promise the taxi was waiting outside and soon delivered her to her flat. She paid the driver and let herself in, pouring a large whisky before slumping into a soft armchair.

What had she done to ask for this complication in her life? she asked herself, still unable to get over the shock of his strangely feeble declaration. What an odd evening it had been with misunderstandings all round. Still, at least the serious part had gone well, with the success of the recital and the promise of a contract in the morning. At least Suzy was on her wavelength even if neither of these two men were.

What a difference there was between them, she mused; Piers with his effeminate ways and quiet unassuming manner, Anton live with energy and virility, an intolerant man who demanded all or nothing. Well, she was best without either of them, except on a professional footing. She needed Piers as a mentor and guide. She needed Anton as she needed any musician already established in such a competitive world, as a stepping-stone for her own advancement. Otherwise, on a personal note, she wanted nothing to do with either of them.

Suzy had arranged a generous deal with the record company to play several Beethoven sonatas on a solo album as well as two Mozart piano concertos with the London Philharmonic Orchestra. Rehearsals for that would start in the autumn, followed closely by two recording sessions. Natasha felt elated as the two women left the studios after signing the agreement. She had said nothing to Suzy about events immediately after her recital, feeling rather embarrassed at her own stupidity.

The day of the piano lesson proved to be inclement, in more ways than one. The weather had broken at last after the long relentless heat-wave, with a violent storm which began in the early hours of the morning. Outside her flat, Natasha hailed a taxi which swung through a deep puddle, soaking her feet and legs. She contemplated rushing in to change, but decided against it in her anxiety to get this meeting with Piers over and done with. It had preyed on her mind ever since his unsolicited advances to her. She wondered how he would behave on this occasion.

'Come in, my darling,' he greeted her in the entrance to his flat. She shuddered, not knowing if she had caught a chill or merely an aversion to him.

Still, she told herself, 'darling' in Piers's vocabulary means nothing. He calls everyone 'darling'. That is one of his traits that annoys me.

'Let me take your coat,' he was saying. She found herself pulling away from his touch. 'Coffee?'

She was comforted by the warmth of the bone-china cup as she wrapped her fingers round it, enjoying the hot liquid thawing her chilled body. Much to her relief, the lesson went smoothly, Piers keeping to his professional role of tutor throughout. It was not until she was preparing to leave that he suddenly altered his behaviour.

'Have you been considering what I said to you the other day?' he purred, catching her unawares as she was about to don her still damp coat.

'I don't remember you saying anything particular,'

she pretended, hoping that would be the end of the matter.

'You must recall, Tasha, my dear,' he went on, placing both hands on her shoulders before she could duck out of his way. 'My affection for you has grown. I think of you night and day; in fact I find I must be in love with you.'

'Piers ...' she began, a pleading note in her voice.

'Say there's a chance you could love me, just a little.'

'Piers,' she tried again. 'You're not my type.'

Something seemed to explode in Piers's head. His face turned puce and his grey eyes grew large and menacing.

'So I'm not your type? After all this time, you admit that, you ungrateful little vixen? And who is your type, eh? Eh?'

He pushed her roughly from him so she fell clumsily against the piano, stunned to silence.

'I'll tell you who is your type: that pretentious sod, Anton Martineau, pushing his way into your life as if he owns you. I've seen the look on your face whenever he is near, or even at the mention of his name.'

How she escaped from Piers's flat she did not know, but minutes later she found herself running wildly through the torrential rain. Not thinking to find a cab, she arrived home drenched to the skin, making for the bathroom, peeling off her dripping clothes as the hot water filled the bath.

What rubbish that man talks, she told herself as she lay back in the soothing water, bubbles forming a cocoon around her. It was just irrational thinking because he's been hurt. As if Anton Martineau was her type! What a ridiculous suggestion. If anything, he managed to bring out the worst in her with his chauvinistic remarks about her piano playing.

Or was it the worst? her other self argued. After all, hadn't she played the best ever following his comments? Hadn't he stimulated her to greater things?

He is very good-looking, she had to admit, and his eyes, such a steely blue, bored into her mind. She closed her eyes, picturing Anton Martineau, towering above her, denying any knowledge of that ill-fated bouquet.

The telephone rang in the other room.

'Damn!' she murmured. Should she let it ring? Whoever it was could try again later. She attempted to shut out the persistent bell, but the caller was very patient. Eventually, her resistance was worn away and she was about to raise herself from the comforting warmth when it stopped.

I'd better get out anyway, she decided, before my thoughts deviate any further in that man's direction. She stood up, wrapping a large bathsheet around her. As she stepped out of the bath the phone began to ring again. Leaving a trail of wet footprints across the carpet, she picked up the receiver. The voice at the other end froze her to the spot.

'Natasha?'

'Yes. Is that Mr ... I mean Anton?'

'It is. Where were you just now? I let the phone ring for aeons, then try again immediately afterwards and you answer.'

'I was in the bath, actually,' she whispered, feeling the heat return to her face and a perplexing tingling all over her body. Why, oh, why did she allow him to have this ridiculous effect on her?

'In the bath?' he repeated. She could detect the smile on his lips as he spoke. 'With whom, may I ask?'

'No, you may not ask,' she returned irritably. 'If you must know, I was out in that deluge and almost drowned. Anyway, how did you find my number?'

She had been ex-directory for a long time, ever since Pete, a former boyfriend, had begun incessantly phoning and pestering her. It had been her last emotional relationship and at the time she had sworn she would not bother with men again. It was too easy to become involved, only to be hurt in one way or another.

'I contacted your agent, Ms Dannovitch.'

'Oh, you mean Suzy.'

She made a mental note to tear Suzy off a strip when she next spoke to her. She had no right to give her number to all and sundry. It was her turn to smile to herself. Fancy calling the great Anton Martineau 'all and sundry'!

Why did he want my number? she wondered, waiting for him to speak. I jolly well hope he doesn't share Piers's opinion and think he's bowled me over. Well, he's got another think coming.

'She advised me to contact you. This is purely a business call, you understand.'

'Oh.'

Natasha chastized herself for ever contemplating any other reason for his call.

'My agent telephoned me earlier today with some bad news. I'm conducting Brahms' Second Piano Concerto tomorrow evening in the Festival Hall.'

'That *is* bad news.' She felt provocative all of a sudden.

'Natasha, I'm being deadly serious.'

'Sorry, but what's it got to do with me?'

'Can you play it?'

'Yes, of course. I know it well. Why?'

'The piano soloist is indisposed. My agent has been unable so far to find anyone to stand in for him. I phoned Ms Dannovitch to ask if you were available at short notice to take his place.'

Natasha swallowed hard. He definitely had changed his opinion of her playing since they first met.

'She said you are free of engagements tomorrow night, but I'd better ask you personally if you would do it.'

Natasha tried to think fast. Why should she jump at his beck and call? But then, it would be excellent for her career prospects. Wasn't that exactly how some people climbed the ladder, by replacing someone at short notice? She would act hard-to-get, let him come down a rung or two, before agreeing to do it.

'Are you still there?'

'Yes.' She tried to sound off-hand, unimpressed.

'Well! Will you do it or not?' He was beginning to sound impatient.

'I'm just weighing up the pros and cons in my mind before I give you my decision.'

'Well!' he exclaimed again. 'There's one thing you're not short of and that's nerve. Most people would give their eye teeth for an opportunity like this.'

'But I'm not "most people", I hope you realize.'

'I'm beginning to, I assure you.'

'Tomorrow night, you said?'

'Yes. Now, Natasha, will you stop playing this silly game with me?'

'OK. After careful consideration, I agree to do it.'

She heard a sigh at the other end of the phone.

'Thank you. I'll call my agent then I'll phone yours and they can draw up details. In the meanwhile I'll tell you that rehearsals are tomorrow morning at ten in the Hall. See you then.'

He finished quite abruptly and she smiled with satisfaction at his annoyance.

'Fifteen all,' she laughed smugly to herself, suddenly realizing she was sitting in a damp towel which had turned rather cold.

In the bedroom, she rubbed hard at her skin to warm herself up. Standing in front of the mirror as she pulled on her scanty underwear, sweater and jeans she was suitably pleased with what she saw, a long shapely body with full, yet pert breasts, trim buttocks and elegant legs. She was particularly satisfied that, after losing over two stone several years ago she had not returned to the plump five-foot-eight image she had hated so much.

She went to the piano to search out her copy of the Brahms. She had boasted to Anton that she knew it well, but that was poetic, or more accurately musical, licence. She would have to practise hard. She found the manuscript and stood it open at the first page on the stand above the keys. She would just phone Suzy to make sure this was official before devoting the rest of the day and evening to music.

There was a ring at the doorbell. Sighing at the interruption, she reluctantly went to the door, finding none other than her friend and agent on the step.

'I was just about to phone you,' laughed Natasha with a hug.

'I just had to come round for a chat. Things are happening so fast in your life I had to make sure your feet are still firmly on the ground. What on earth have you been saying?'

'To Anton Martineau, do you mean?'

'Well, yes, him for a start. When he phoned back to say you'd agreed to do the Brahms, he was in a foul mood.'

'I'm afraid I scored in the game of one-upmanship.'

'I'm not surprised he was mad then. It's a wonder he didn't cancel his offer. You'd better be careful.'

'Rubbish. He deserved every single bit of it. Anyway, Suzy, you said "him for a start". Who else do you mean?'

She suddenly knew what Suzy was going to say.

'Piers.'

Natasha learned how Piers had spoken to Suzy almost as soon as she had left his flat.

'He was in a terrible state, a cross between a whimper and an explosion. You'd better tell me your side of the story, as his was confusing, to say the least.'

Natasha related the short sequence of events that had taken place since the recital. Suzy nodded, frowned and laughed in turn.

'And he actually accused you of fancying Anton Martineau?'

'Of all the unlikely candidates.'

Suzy gave her a knowing look.

'I had only just put the receiver down when the great man himself was on the phone for the first time. You know why, of course. After my ear bending session with Piers I thought the only thing to do was pass Anton straight on to you. Perhaps it would have been safer for me to have dealt with him myself. Anything for a quiet life! So you're going to do the Brahms, even after so short a time since you swore you'd never play under his baton again?'

'I had to think of my career.'

'Tash, you old liar. Perhaps there's a shred of truth

in Piers's accusation.'

Natasha suddenly disappeared into the kitchen to put the kettle on, but not before Suzy had spotted her friend's discomfort.

'Hmm,' mused the agent to herself. She hoped Tasha was not going to make a fool of herself with this powerful man, who was never short of female companions.

'Take care,' she teased as the client emerged with two steaming cups.

'You're as bad as the rest,' retorted Natasha. 'My association with that man is purely and simply professional. No more.'

In bed later that night, her bravado of the day gave way to misgivings. She had been an idiot to reject Piers's advances quite so tactlessly, thus estranging herself from a kind and valued tutor. She presumed that to continue lessons with Piers was out of the question, which meant finding someone else. That might be difficult at this important stage in her career.

Different thoughts dominated her mind, however, as the immediacy of the next confrontation with Anton became apparent. She wished she had not been quite so flippant with him, especially since hearing his frame of mind when he spoke to Suzy afterwards. He was bound to take it out on her in rehearsal as he did last time, making a laughing stock out of her to the entire orchestra. Why had she not had the courage to refuse to do the concert?

Don't be silly, she reprimanded herself not for the first time. Nothing could have flattered you more than a direct request from the maestro. You leapt at the chance. It was your fault that he saw red.

She had disciplined herself after Suzy had gone to studying the piece which she was to play the following day. Confident that she had mastered it sufficiently well, her only dread remained in meeting Anton face to face.

His tactics, however, were to ignore Natasha entirely when she arrived slightly early next morning. She had found her way through the artists' entrance, up in the lift to the third floor as instructed by the official on duty at the window, to the soloist's room. This was another first, performing this time in the Festival Hall. Three new venues in less than a month wasn't bad, she tried to convince herself as she sat alone, avidly studying her music, waiting for the time she would be required up on the stage.

'You're wanted now, lovey,' smiled the messenger, seeing the nervous figure curled up in a chair. 'You all right?'

'Yes, thank you. Could you direct me to the stage, please?'

'I'll do better than that. I'll take you there myself.'

She was led through a maze of corridors and steps that she was convinced she would never remember again. She climbed the flight of stairs that took her up on to the stage and felt all eyes on her as she approached the piano. Several members of the orchestra welcomed her pleasantly, but she could not rid herself of that same feeling of the little-girl-lost that she had experienced on her first day at her new secondary school many years ago.

Without any opportunity to relax, Natasha found herself propelled into the music with no more than what she might describe as a dirty look from the conductor. Beyond the necessary contact between musicians, he gave her no encouragement whatsoever and several times she fumbled the notes, becoming more and more despondent as the piano concerto progressed.

As she approached her room for the coffee interval, he hissed behind her,

'I thought you said you knew this very well. Too many mistakes so far.'

'If you could see your way to being humane or even human towards me, I'd probably do a lot better.'

'Can't stand the heat, eh?'

He went into his room and slammed the door.

Oh dear, definitely a point to him, she pondered. I can't let him browbeat me. I overcame his attitude last time, and I'll do it again.

Determination burned in her eyes as she sat prepared to begin again after the break. There was a light tap on her shoulder and she turned towards the leader of the orchestra behind her.

'*Courage, ma brave*," he grinned. 'We're all great fans of yours, you know. Don't be so scared. Enjoy yourself.'

'Thank you, Charles,' she smiled back. 'I'll try.'

'OK, everyone?' Another, impatient voice cut the air and Natasha glanced up to find his demand was directed straight at her.

She smiled assent and liked the effect it had on his austere approach, the frown melting from his face.

The final part of rehearsal was in complete contrast to earlier mediocrity and Anton rewarded the pianist with a passing word on his way out.

'You seem to rise to the occasion,' he whispered close to her ear. 'I shall have to annoy you more often.'

She tried to read his look, but his face was inscrutable.

'Keep it up, Natasha,' said the leader as they left the stage together. 'It'll be all right on the night, just you see.'

The image of Anton's face plagued her for the rest of the day. She had to admit he intrigued her, with his aggressive attitude mixed with that enigmatic demeanour, and her determination was strengthened to even the score.

It must be all wrong, she reprimanded herself, to be motivated to do well for these reasons. Personalities should not be part of it. But she was afraid that, in this case, they were.

She managed to snatch two hours sleep late in the afternoon and she was in a positive frame of mind by the time Suzy called to fetch her. It seemed a little disconcerting that Piers was not there to wish her luck before going on to play, but she was secretly relieved at his absence. What would she have done if he had been there? It would have sent her into a spin and multiplied her concert nerves.

'Good luck!' Suzy hugged her as she left the soloist's room to head for the hall. 'I have every confidence in you, but don't forget, you're still out to prove yourself.'

Too right, mused Natasha when her friend had departed. This is just as big an opportunity as the Tchaikovsky to prove myself to the public. And to Maesto Martineau himself!

An hour later, Natasha found herself surrounded by a throng of well-wishers, who filled her little room and spilled out into the corridor. Many people had come in search of what the newspaper critics deemed to be 'the new star in the musical heavens' and she was overwhelmed at such a response from the public.

Men and women of all ages waited patiently for a turn to be near her, some requesting autographs, others merely wanting to be able to tell their friends that they had seen her in person. One old man desperately wanted to relate his life story and had to be politely thanked and moved on.

Suzy stood loyally at her side throughout the tiring, yet exhilarating time, smiling in the knowledge that she, Suzy Dannovitch, had helped in her client's success. Only a tiny part of her glowed with the realization that this could make a difference to her permanent financial crisis. Fifteen per cent of a client's earnings could add up to a small fortune.

The crowd thinned at last, enabling the two women to sit down and relax, heaving sighs of relief and pleasure.

'Well! How about that? Who'd have imagined little old me standing here like royalty holding court?'

'I'm so excited for you, Tash. I feel my breath taken away. It's all happening at once.'

'We must go out and celebrate. Where shall we go?'

Several members of the orchestra popped their heads round the door to add their words of congratulation.

'I said you'd be fine once you regained your confidence.' The orchestra leader shook her warmly by the hand. 'And don't you let anyone, I repeat, anyone, knock it again.' He winked broadly and Natasha laughed at his reference.

'Thanks, Charles. I won't – not anyone!'

'What did he mean?' asked Suzy when they were alone again.

'Only something he said to me in rehearsal when

our great man was beginning to gain dominance in
our game of one-upmanship. I think I just about won
that point. Thirty all, we are now.'

'Is he still harassing you?'

'Is who still harassing you?' asked a deep voice from
the doorway.

Both ladies quelled a desire to giggle, not wanting
to witness the irascible side of this man.

'Nobody you'd recognize,' said Suzy hurriedly.

Natasha smiled gratefully at her. He would certainly not admit to recognizing himself as anything
but perfect, she was sure.

'You had quite a following tonight, Miss Spitzen,' he
said coolly. 'Not without justification, I might add.'

'Generous praise, Mr Martineau. Thank you.'

'I could go so far as to add that you play Brahms as
well as you do Tchaikovsky.'

A warm smile flashed across her face and he returned the smile, wilting her resolve to avoid any
more than the minimum contact with him. She held
his gaze for a moment, recognizing open approval for
once.

'Ms Dannovitch?' A voice called from somewhere
outside the room. Suzy went in answer and peered out
into the corridor.

'I won't be a minute,' she turned and said to Natasha.
'I have to see someone.'

With a wave she was gone, leaving Natasha alone
with Anton, whose presence now seemed to dominate
the room, his masculinity a potent force over her.

She's done this to me on purpose, Natasha cursed.
It was a ploy to leave us alone together, the match-
making hussy. She arranged for that call, I know she
did.

'You're lost for words,' Anton was saying, his voice calm, almost hypnotic. 'Not shy, are you?'

Natasha laughed too loudly, still unable to think of anything to say.

'I was in the middle of paying you a compliment, before we were so rudely interrupted.'

'So you were. Thank you.'

'I thought I wouldn't repeat my behaviour to you after the Prom, when I ignored you after such an outstanding performance.'

'Partly my fault,' she stumbled. 'I expect I asked for it.'

'Most unprofessional of me, I admit.'

'And me.'

'Look, I'm not finding this any easier than you are. I'm not quite as bad as the impression I have set you. Let me make amends. How about dinner tomorrow night?'

Desperately, Natasha searched her mind for an excuse. First Piers, then Suzy, had tried to suggest a liaison between her and Anton and she did not want it. No more men, was the promise she had made to herself, and this one had a reputation with the women, too.

'Chez Sandrine? You like French cuisine?'

The refusal on her lips determined not to be heard.

'Eight o'clock, tomorrow evening then. I'll pick you up outside your flat. Till tomorrow.'

Helpless, she watched his elegant back as he departed.

'Thank you very much, Suzy,' she seethed as her friend re-entered the room. 'I'm trapped into eating a meal with him tomorrow night. I blame this entirely on you.'

'I bet you'll think of some reason you can't make it.'

'No. Don't you worry. To spite the lot of you and prove you all wrong, I shall have to go through with it.'

Three

'*Bonsoir, M Martineau*. Your table.'

They were led through an elegant reception room, decorated in Edwardian style, and up an ornate flight of stairs to one side. Their table was situated at the far end of the upper room, in a corner, beneath a fluted glass bowl lamp. A silver vase containing a single dusk-pink rose adorned the centre of the circular damask-clad table.

Anton, the perfect gentleman, stepped lightly ahead of Natasha to pull the balloon-backed chair away from the table, pushing it gently as she sat down. She watched him as he spoke quietly with the waiter, who obviously knew him rather well and accepted his tip in an ingratiating manner.

This must be the place he brings all his prospective conquests, she thought wryly to herself.

As Anton made himself comfortable opposite her, Natasha viewed the remainder of the room, quite long and narrow with the stairs coming up about halfway along one edge. She counted a dozen tables, mainly set for two, and, beyond the stairwell she spotted a grand piano, probably a Boudoir Grand, she guessed. Its lid was closed and a massive aspidistra stood proudly in the centre. Various other tropical plants were placed throughout the restaurant, serving as screens between the tables.

'You approve of my choice?'

She turned her face to him, unable to avoid noticing the flattering effect the subdued lighting had on his features.

'Very chic,' she replied, wondering if that was the correct word to use for such a place. 'Yes,' she added self-consciously, 'I do.'

A large menu written entirely in French was placed before her and she smiled acknowledgement to the waiter. She studied the list of fare for several minutes before raising her eyes to find Anton scrutinizing her with an amused expression on his handsome face.

He thinks I'm floored by this menu, she chuckled inwardly. He's underestimated my talents though.

'Do you need any help?' he was saying. 'I'll translate if you wish.'

'I'll have escargots to start with, please, followed by the fillet of sole in butter.'

His face had altered almost imperceptibly, but she could read in his eyes the surprise at her competence.

'You understand French?'

'*Mais, bien sûr, monsieur.*' It was her turn to show laughter in her eyes while he avidly contemplated the menu.

'I'll have snails, too. I love them, soaked in garlic butter and herbs, followed by the lamb.'

He had recovered well. Natasha felt her mouth watering at his description of the starter they had both decided to have.

'You forget I studied at Paris Conservatoire.'

'Of course. And you lived in Paris?'

'In the suburbs, actually. Maison Lafitte. Do you know it?'

'I've heard of it.'

'I lived with a lovely family and although I had a

passing knowledge of schoolgirl French before I arrived, the only real way to learn it is to have to speak it all the time. It's a bit rusty now, but it's like riding a bicycle – once achieved, never forgotten!'

She gained in confidence once she had established herself as possessing more than a few grey cells between her ears, as Suzy would have put it. She hoped this would be reflected in the way he treated her from now on. A little more respect, for a start, she deserved.

'An aperitif, Madame?'

She smiled disarmingly up at the waiter and shook her head.

'No, thank you. I prefer to stick to wine.'

'OK, Gaston. No aperitifs tonight.' He turned to Natasha. 'Would you prefer a dry white wine with your fish?'

'I'm happy with red, if you'd like it with your meat.'

'That settles it. We'll have a bottle of Muscadet to begin with – that'll complement the snails. Then Beaujolais with the main course and you can drink which you choose.'

Natasha concurred. She was not a connoisseur of wines, as her student finances had always restricted her to the house wines, sold by the carafe. She knew she liked both that Anton had picked, however.

They had travelled by taxi to the restaurant in the heart of the West End, Anton leaving his silver Audi outside her apartment.

'Partly the parking problem,' he had explained, 'but also the drink/drive laws. I'm not willing to risk losing my licence.'

At the back of her mind, Natasha had wondered what he intended doing about getting home after dropping her off, but assumed he would continue in the same taxi. She definitely knew where he would not be. Her doors were barred, let there be no mistake on that subject, and if he for one moment presumed otherwise....

The Muscadet was perfectly chilled, cooling Natasha in the rising temperature of the restaurant. The room had filled since their arrival and although all the windows hung open, the oppressive heat of the past weeks seemed to have returned. A pianist had begun to play and she recognized the French composers she knew so well. The music completed the picture of Edwardian grandeur the proprietor attempted to portray.

'Delicious,' she murmured in answer to the waiter's enquiry. She was engrossed in dipping tiny pieces of light French bread into the melted butter.

'Bad for the heart,' laughed Anton, sharing her enjoyment in the same activity. 'It's a wonder the entire French population doesn't die of heart failure at a young age.'

'Some say that red wine counteracts that,' she replied. 'You know in many families, the children drink diluted red wine with their meals from quite young.'

'Perhaps there is a modicum of truth in that. We can put it to the test.'

He signalled to the discreetly hovering waiter.

'We'll have the Beaujolais now, if you would.'

Natasha realized with horror that the Muscadet bottle was empty. Had she drunk half of it? It had certainly been very welcome and had slipped down easily. She had been aware of Gaston recharging her glass a few times. She would have to restrict her consumption of the red.

'I have to admit I have enjoyed working with you.'

Natasha met his eyes steadily, but read no sarcasm or humour.

'Thanks. Do you always inspire soloists in the same way?'

'I did attempt to explain that yesterday, hence this meal to make up for my attitude towards you. I could ask you a similar question, of course – are you always such a little spitfire?'

'I hope not. I was provoked, I suppose.'

'Play your cards right and you're guaranteed a full international career from now on.'

'What do you mean, play my cards right?' She thought she recognized danger signs in that phrase. It sounded as if there might be strings attached.

'Get your agent to work hard for you, to capitalize on your recent success.'

'She already does, I assure you.'

'And find a good teacher.'

'Now you mention it....'

She told Anton of a difference of opinion that had lost her Piers as a tutor. She omitted to mention the cause.

'I'll see what I can do.'

The Beaujolais bottle had mysteriously emptied itself and she was suddenly aware of a swimming sensation in her head. She felt relaxed and happy, finding how easy it was to talk to this man she had labelled with a large chauvinist sticker. She spoke of her mother in Devon and discovered he had grandparents near her.

He talked of brothers and sisters in various places spread over the world. She had never thought of him as having family. He had always given the impression he was too sophisticated to admit to a family!

He showed interest in her brother, Tom, in Canada and she was proud to boast of his success in the field of computers.

'Coffee, *Monsieur, Madame* ?'

Natasha looked at her watch. Past eleven o'clock? How was that possible? The sole had been superb and she had followed it with a pear charlotte with raspberry sauce that could only be described as decadent. She felt replete. She did not really think she had room for even a small cup of coffee.

'I don't feel I could,' she apologized. 'You have one if you'd like one.'

'Thank you, but no, Gaston. Just the bill.'

Anton tipped the waiter again as they left. He had shown a perfect balance, between attentive and discreet.

'*Merci, Monsieur.* See you soon.'

In the back of the taxi, Natasha leaned snugly against the cushioned seat, conscious of this attractive man who had treated her to a delicious meal. He had more than compensated for his previous behaviour towards her and she was all too aware of a growing physical attraction for him. She enjoyed the firm muscular feel of his shoulder through his thin summer-weight jacket, realizing that this was the first contact they had had, apart from his theatrical appraisal of her in front of a full concert hall.

Too soon, the taxi slowed to a standstill and she recognized her apartment in the darkness, unwelcoming with its black windows. She had forgotten to leave a light on. She hated going into a dark flat alone at night.

'Would you like me to accompany you to your door?'

She nodded, her head still spinning as she did so.

'Wait here,' she heard him instruct the taxi driver. 'I'll be a couple of minutes.'

A strong arm round her waist steadied Natasha, but at the same time made her weak with the sensation that spread throughout her body. She searched for her key which she gave to Anton, watching his powerful hands insert it in the lock. She wanted this moment to never end.

"Coffee?' she heard her own voice say from somewhere in the distance.

'Why not?'

He pushed open the door for her to enter.

'I'll pay off the taxi.'

What was she doing? she wondered as she contentedly filled the kettle and plugged it in. Asking for trouble, no doubt. But at that moment she did not care. She wanted trouble, if it was in the form of this example of male perfection.

She heard the flat door close, knowing Anton had joined her in the kitchen, overwhelmed by the proximity of his body behind her. She felt his eyes studying her back and she turned to face him. He averted his gaze abruptly.

'In here?' he asked, walking in the direction of the lounge.

Perhaps I'm a fool to have invited him in, she thought. He's regretting it already.

She made two black coffees, put them on a tray with the bowl of sugar then followed him. He was standing with his back to her, studying some photographs on the dresser. She put the tray down on the low table and sank into cushions of the sofa as he came to join her.

'My family,' she explained, nodding in the direction of the photographs.

'Yes. Very pleasant.'

There was silence between them, Natasha trying desperately to think of something to say, to recapture the intimacy of the evening.

'I ...' they both began together.

'Sorry!' she stammered. 'After you.'

'I was going to say I ought to be going. It's late.'

'As you wish,' she sighed, not knowing whether to be disappointed or relieved.

'I've enjoyed the evening immensely.'

'Me, too. Thank you, Anton.'

They stood up and walked to the door.

'I'll hail another cab. There'll be plenty still around. I'll fetch my car in the morning.'

Gently, he reached out his index finger and lifted her chin. Leaning forward, he touched his lips to hers for a second, then opening the door swiftly, he was gone.

'You two-faced little madam,' Suzy's voice rang loudly down the receiver. Natasha winced, holding the phone away from her to reduce the volume. A drum pounded incessantly in her head.

'I came round to call on you about eleven this morning, and guess whose car was sitting blatantly outside your flat? I was the soul of discretion and went straight home again. Is he still there, or has he gone now?'

Natasha groaned. Not only did she regret the amount of alcohol she had consumed last night, but also her stupidity. The more she remembered of her behaviour towards Anton, the more she hated herself. She had blatantly thrown herself at him. Thank goodness he had seen sense and gone home when he had, or she might have had more to regret!

'Shut up, Suzy!' she whispered, each word vibrating in her brain. 'You're out of order.'

'Don't try denying everything. It won't work. He won you over, admit it. You couldn't resist him.'

'I said shut up,' she shouted painfully.

'Sorry!' Suzy sounded hurt.

'No, he's not here. Hasn't been since about midnight. I feel awful. Look, come round, will you? I'd rather speak to you face to face, then you'll believe me.'

Ten minutes later Natasha had made herself her first black coffee of the day.

'His car's gone,' were Suzy's opening words.

'I suppose I must explain everything to you in words of one syllable. He left his car here so he could drink wine. He came in for a short while then went home in a cab. That's all.'

'And you mean to say nothing at all happened between you?'

Natasha's mournful face softened her friend's attack.

'Promise you'll say nothing to anyone?'

'Cross my heart.'

Suzy listened patiently as she poured out the entire story.

'I feel so ashamed,' she sobbed as she finished. 'He must have thought what a pathetic little pushover I must be. Either that or a loose woman. But I've well and truly blotted my copybook now.'

'He said he'd be in touch?'

'Yes, but I can't imagine he'll want to see me again.

As I know full well, he's never without an endless choice of female talent to choose from.'

'And the kiss he gave you? What was that like?'

For a moment, Natasha's lips tingled with the memory of that short physical contact. She shrugged her shoulders.

'I don't know. Gentle, but probably final.'

'Time will tell,' said Suzy, trying to be helpful. 'I've got more details of future engagements. Do you feel up to it?'

By the time Suzy left, Natasha's head was reeling for other reasons, trying to take in the reams of information about concerts, recitals, recordings, photo sessions and interviews her agent had arranged in the next few months. She was feeling much better, though, about her exploits of the previous evening. She was able to see everything much more in perspective. The best solution was to forget the whole thing, renew her determination to avoid emotional involvement, and concentrate on her music.

For the next few weeks she held herself to her promise, disciplining her time between practising and performing, keeping regular hours and minimizing her intake of alcohol. She had to admit she missed Piers's invaluable guidance, and Suzy made a few enquiries to arrange for a new tutor. Each performance she gave received the same accolade as before both in the press and from her fellow musicians.

She particularly enjoyed working in the studio, though she wondered if it was because of the novelty of the situation, and the making of the discs went well. The solo album came first and after rehearsal, everyone was delighted that the initial take was as near perfect as they could hope. The piano concertos with orchestra took longer, though she became fascinated by the technology behind the mix of sound that was achieved.

From Anton, she heard nothing. There was no reason why he should want to see her again. She had accepted that a long while ago, though she did show more than a usual interest in his whereabouts. He was working abroad, she learned, a tour of Scandinavia as guest conductor to the national orchestras of Sweden, Norway, Finland and Denmark. He was a busy man, much in demand, as he consolidated his position as an internationally acclaimed conductor.

So Natasha was taken aback, one lunchtime, as she took a deserved rest from her piano, to receive a call from the great man himself.

'I think I have some good news for you,' he began. 'Can we meet? I'll fill you in with the details then.'

'When?'

'Now if you're free. The Crooked Billet, near you, in an hour?'

She arrived at the inn before him in the end, after a wild panic to be ready on time. She bought a bitter lemon at the bar and took it into the garden from which she had a vantage point overlooking the car-park.

From the moment she had phoned off, the nerves of old had taken her over as she showered and washed her hair, indecisive about what to wear, curious about what he had to say. Finally, having patted the moisture from her body and lightly moussed her hair, allowing it to dry in its natural waves, she chose a sleeveless white blouse with her navy culottes and sandals. She did not want to appear overdressed for the occasion. The hot weather had extended into a glorious Indian summer, well into October.

After several minutes she witnessed the silver Audi swing into the car-park and the striking figure of Anton Martineau lock the car and walk towards the bar. Dismissing the temptation to rush to meet him, she held her advantage and waited until he came to join her.

'You already have a drink? Have you been waiting long?'

'Not long.'

'Would you like another?'

She glanced at her glass which was almost empty.

'Bitter lemon, please.'

He returned with the drinks.

'Keeping off the alcohol?'

She felt her hackles rise in annoyance. He had touched a nerve, to be sure.

'Sorry. I didn't mean it like that. I wasn't going to mention our previous date. Trust me to get it wrong from the start.'

'I'm sorry, too, about that evening. What must you have thought of me? I've chastised myself many a time for that.'

'We were both to blame, carried away by the occasion, which I truly enjoyed, incidentally.'

'So did I, every moment of it.'

'Every moment?' He stressed the first word.

She nodded and grinned sheepishly.

'Thank goodness that's cleared the air a little. Now we can get back to business and the reason I phoned you.'

That put me in my place, she thought resignedly. No possibility of any developments in this relationship. It was exactly what he had said, a meal to make amends, and there was the end of it.

'You mentioned you were in need of a new piano teacher?'

So that was it. She nodded.

'I think I've found someone who would be interested, someone who has been impressed with your playing and has followed your progress and rise to fame over the past few years.'

He reached in his pocket and produced a card. She gasped. Norman Flaxman had been a brilliant pianist in his time, until illness had curtailed his playing career. If she had been a violinist and Yehudi Menuhin had shown interest in her, she could not have been more delighted.

'He wants to meet you if you agree.'

'Agree? I'm deeply flattered. When?'

'So that's about it, Mummy,' she finished, a week later on one of her frequent visits to the West Country. 'I'm to start with Norman Flaxman in November, for a trial period initially. He was charm itself, though not a flatterer by any means. As Anton said, he has shown interest in me for long enough to have recognized my faults too. I'm really grateful to Anton to have arranged the meeting.'

'And Anton? What about him? You're obviously smitten with him.'

'Mummy! Will you kindly not be match-maker or I shan't tell you anything at all. He's a very attractive man, as you can see from photographs of him, but I'm small fry in his eyes and you know my feeling about men.'

'But Pete was years ago, Tasha. Don't let that cloud

the rest of your life, please.'

Weeks passed, with Natasha leading an increasingly busy life. After her trial sessions with Norman Flaxman, they signed a long-term agreement and she soon realized how helpful his advice became. Suzy built up a full schedule for her, leaving time for her regular return to Devon. Her mother's health was fading fast and Natasha gave strict instructions to Suzy to keep enough free time for this. She would never forgive herself if she ever put her mother to the end of her list of priorities.

One evening, when Mrs Spitzen had gone to bed early, Natasha decided to pay a visit to the village pub. It had been her regular haunt in her teens and many of her old friends still lived in the area. Perhaps there would be someone there that she knew. She kissed her mother goodnight, told her where she was heading, what time she would be back, and left the house. It was only a hundred yards or so to the pub so she walked briskly through the village in the chill night air.

Head down, she did not notice the sleek silver car parked at the side of the pub, or she might not have ventured in. Entering the public bar, she was greeted with open arms by several old acquaintances and she spent an enjoyable hour chatting over old times.

'I must get back,' she said suddenly. 'I promised Mummy. Just in case she needs me.'

A familiar voice from the saloon bar made her stop dead in her tracks. There was no mistaking the deep, impelling tone. She heard laughter, a woman's voice, and she could not resist peering round the screen that separated the two bars.

'Natasha,' he called with exaggerated enthusiasm. 'What brings you here?'

'I might ask the same of you. I've come to see my mother.'

'Of course, and I my grandparents. What a coincidence.'

He came round to join her.

'Natasha, may I introduce my, er, second cousin, Maria. Maria, Natasha.'

Second cousin, my foot, she thought.

'I don't mean to be rude, but I really have to go. I left my mother alone and she's unwell.'

'Let me buy you a drink, just a quick one. Brian, something for Miss Spitzen.'

Trust him to be on Christian name terms with the publican.

'All right. Half of bitter, please.'

Just let him dare to mention her alcohol intake, that's all! The atmosphere was tense between them. She finished the beer as quickly as decency allowed.

'Thanks, Anton,' she said, forcing a smile, 'but I must go now.'

'Can I give you a lift?'

'No thanks, it's only a few yards.'

She slipped out before he could insist and reached her mother's house at a trot. Letting herself in, she went straight upstairs, the scream escaping from her lips before she reached the landing. There lay her mother, stretched out in front of her, deathly pale, her breathing laboured.

What should she do? Pick her up? Phone for the ambulance? But that would take ages to reach here. The nearest ambulance station was at least ten miles away, then the trip to the hospital would be a further twelve.

On impulse she ran out into the road. A car was approaching, picking up speed. Frantically, she waved her arms and the car slewed to a standstill.

'What the hell?' demanded an angry voice.

'Anton! Thank God it's you. Quick! It's my mother.'

'Where?' he shouted, recognizing the urgency in her voice, as he entered the house.

'On the landing.'

'Maria,' he ordered as he saw the prostrate woman, 'phone the police. Tell them who we are and where we are. Tell them I'm heading for Exeter General – no time to wait for an ambulance.'

He had already lifted Mrs Spitzen gently in his arms and was heading down the stairs.

'Describe my car and ask them to meet me *en route* and give me an escort for the rest of the journey.'

He had reached the front door. Natasha stared in alarm at her mother as she struggled to breathe.

'Ask them to prepare the hospital for an emergency – any details you can think of – then call a cab and get yourself home. I'll phone you.'

Natasha wrenched open the rear door of the Audi and climbed in. As carefully as speed would allow, Anton handed the stricken woman into her daughter's arms, and leapt into the driver's seat.

Within a mile or two of a terrifying journey, where Anton exceeded the speed limit by many times along narrow country lanes, Natasha heard the siren of the police car that sped to join them. Anton leaned on the horn to indicate the desperate need to hurry then followed the tail lights of the police escort.

'Hang on, Mummy, please,' Natasha whispered

time and time again into the gasping woman's ear, kissing her cheek continually.

Eventually, she could see the welcoming lights of the hospital and the convoy swung in through the gates and up to the casualty department. The reception committee wasted no time in transferring Mrs Spitzen on to a trolley, equipped with breathing apparatus which they put to use immediately. She was taken straight into intensive care, leaving Natasha and Anton in the waiting-room.

'It's serious, isn't it?' she asked rhetorically. 'I must phone Tom, in Canada. He must catch the first flight home.'

She found a booth, thankful that she had memorized her brother's number. She prayed he would be at home. She pressed out the digits with shaking fingers. There was a series of clicks then a telephone ringing remarkably clearly. A woman's voice answered.

'Sally, is that you?'

'Yes?'

'It's Tasha here. Is Tom in?'

'No. He's at work.'

'It's Mummy. She's dying; I'm sure of it. She's in intensive care in Exeter hospital. We've just rushed her here.'

'Look Tasha. I'll call him at the office and tell him. You phone back in half an hour and I'll let you know what he plans to do.'

A nurse walked through the waiting area.

'Miss Spitzen?'

Natasha put down the phone and waved at the nurse.

'Yes? That's me.'

Natasha filled in a few of her mother's details on a

form the nurse handed to her.

'How is she?'

'Poorly, I have to be honest. The doctor will have a word with you shortly.'

'Can I see her?'

'Not at present. We're trying to make her more comfortable. We'll let you know.'

A woman in a white coat approached, holding out her hand, which Natasha shook solemnly.

'What are her chances, Doctor?'

'Not good. She may last the night, but I have to be honest with you, her condition is critical.'

Natasha made her way back to the phone booth. Almost half an hour had elapsed since her last call, and she felt sure Sally must have contacted Tom by now.

'Sal, I was right. She may not last the night. Tom's got to come.'

'OK, Tash. Keep calm. There's a flight that leaves Vancouver in two hours. I have already booked Tom on it. He can just make it if he leaves now. He should be with you this time tomorrow. He said. "Tell her to hang on, Tash. I'm on my way".'

As Natasha replaced the receiver, she began to shake all over. The events of the evening had happened so fast she had not had time to think, and she had felt calm in the face of emergency, but now, as the worst was about to begin, she suddenly could not cope.

She turned appealingly to the tall figure whom she realized had been at her side all along.

'Oh, Anton,' she cried as she closed her eyes. The next moment she found comfort, as he held her securely in his strong embrace.

Four

'Oh, Tom! Thank goodness you're here,' she sobbed against her brother's shoulder twenty-four hours later. 'I told her to hang on. I kept praying she would, but in the end she had to let go.'

Tom wiped his eyes.

'If only I could have got here sooner. Why did I have to live so far away?'

They were standing in the hall of their mother's house where Tom had arrived by taxi a few minutes earlier. He had telephoned the hospital from Heathrow so he was already acquainted with the sad news. The sister had also told him that Natasha had left the hospital so he had guessed where he would find her.

They walked to the kitchen and Natasha put the kettle on.

'Will it help you to tell me everything? I'd like you to, if you can bear it.'

She nodded, making two mugs of coffee and sitting down opposite her brother at the kitchen-table.

'I didn't realize quite how much worse she had become or I wouldn't have gone down to the pub,' she sighed. 'Mummy didn't say. I would have been able to call the doctor if I had been here.'

'You can't blame yourself, now then.'

'I can't help it.'

Natasha dissolved in tears again and it was only when she had dried her eyes that Tom spoke.

'Now, Tasha. No more blame. Tell me all.'

Obediently, Natasha managed to relate the events of the evening from her visit to the pub.

'It was a lucky coincidence that Anton Martineau was there. I don't know what I would have done without him.'

Despite the gravity of the situation, Tom smiled to himself. Hadn't his mother written to him only three weeks previously in her last letter, saying how she suspected her daughter of taking a fancy to this handsome conductor! Their mother always had been very astute.

Natasha continued her story. She told of Anton's mastery on finding Mrs Spitzen on the landing, of the car journey, of how she tore herself reluctantly from the comfort of Anton's arms to follow the nurse along the corridors to the little room and her mother's bedside. She told of how she had stared at the machines and tubes that were seemingly keeping their mother alive, of long hopeless hours through the night, of the end coming peacefully at dawn.

'She didn't once open her eyes during that time, but she knew I was there. I held her hand the whole time and talked to her about you and me and Daddy, and several times I felt a slight squeeze.'

'How did you get home?' asked Tom, swallowing the lump in his throat. 'By taxi?'

'No! You won't believe this, but I was just about to leave the hospital when a nurse came in with a message for me. Anton had waited there all night and had just heard that Mummy had died.'

Tom gave her a knowing look.

'He brought me home,' she went on, seeming not to notice her brother's expression. 'He persuaded me to

drink some whisky and made us both some breakfast.
I can't quite make him out. I thought he was an
absolute pig when I first met him, but he couldn't have
done more.'

'How long did he stay?'

'When he was sure I would be OK on my own he left,
saying he would be in touch. I suppose that was mid
morning. He even phoned this evening to check I was
all right.'

'You like him, don't you?'

'I have to confess, I'm afraid I do.'

The next week was a fraught one for Natasha. First,
she had to phone Suzy to ask her to cancel any
engagements, then she and Tom embarked on all the
necessary funeral arrangements, including notifying
the rest of the fairly extensive family. She had not
time to think of anything but the immediate future
and the subject of Anton did not recur until the night
before the funeral. It was Tom who introduced his
name.

'Have you let Anton know when the funeral is?'

'No. He won't want to come. He didn't know Mummy.'

'I suppose not.'

To their surprise, however, and Natasha's embarrassment, his familiar broad back was evident at the
rear of the chapel as they followed the coffin down the
aisle.

'I had to see it through," he confessed to Natasha
afterwards at the house. 'I felt involved, you see. Why
didn't you let me know?'

Natasha did not answer. She felt her emotions were
too mixed up to try and explain anything to herself, let
alone anyone else and least of all, him. She had not

wanted him to see her grief and yet had been relieved
to see him there.

After Tom had suggested notifying him, her mind
had been racing confusedly over their so-called relationship. She could count on her fingers the number of
times they had met and yet it was as if she had known
him for a long time. He had seen her in her most
vulnerable state on more than one occasion and now,
although she did not hate him any more, she still felt
a form of resentment that he had the advantage over
her.

Fortunately, he was one of the first to leave, allowing Natasha to relax with the family gathered about
her.

'Who was that young man?' asked her old great
aunt. 'He looked vaguely familiar.'

'He's a conductor, Aunty, that's why you've seen
him before. He was only here because it was he who
took Mummy to hospital the night she died.'

'I don't think that was the only reason,' whispered
Tom in her ear. 'You realize that, don't you, sis?'

Getting back into the routine of work was not easy for
Natasha after the trauma of her stay in Devon. She
had also found time to get to know her brother again.
He had been in Canada for five years and they had
only met on three occasions during that time, apart
from rather infrequent phone calls to one another. His
life over the other side of the world sounded idyllic to
Natasha as she listened avidly to his description of his
flat in the city, the cottage on Vancouver Island, the
yacht and the rounds of parties with friends and
business associates.

'You've no excuse now, have you? At last, you can

visit us and be paid for it! Your fare and hotel bill will come out of expenses for the concerts. Leave your entertainment to me.'

Natasha felt excited at the prospect of a trip to Canada that was now only a few months away.

'You will come with me on this trip, won't you?' she asked Suzy when she was back in London working hard on some new pieces for her next engagement.

'I wouldn't miss it for the world!' laughed Suzy. 'As long as Tom promises he'll provide us with some handsome male escorts – rich, of course.'

'How much free time have we both got around then?'

Suzy consulted her diary for the next year.

'Well, you've got nothing during the week before the concerts, but that will be for rehearsals. You have three concerts in the second week. Then your next engagement is almost three weeks later in London.'

'And you?'

'Oh, there's no problem there. As long as I organize everybody else before we go, I can spare up to three weeks. I haven't had a holiday for two years. I deserve the break.'

'Great! I'll tell Tom of your demands on the male front!'

She spoke to Tom later that night.

'You got back all right then?'

'Yes. Thought the flight would never end, though. I think we must have had the wind against us.'

Natasha laughed.

'Hey. That's better, little sister. I've been worried about you. You've looked so pale and drawn. Have you talked to Suzy about coming over?'

'Yes, but she'll only come if you provide us with rich

handsome males.'

'No problem. You'll have them queuing up. I'll fix you both up, you can be sure.'

Natasha sat quietly for some time after she had rung off. For all her cheerful exterior to Tom and her message from Suzy, she was not at all enthusiastic about an endless procession of masculinity. Her mind went back again to Pete who had hurt her so badly, to Piers whom she had rejected, and to Anton.

She closed her eyes and tried to shut him out of her thoughts. She recalled his eyes, deep, penetrating blue, that sent messages she could not understand. She pictured his golden hair and strong nose, his full lips that had once brushed hers, his strong arms that had held her so surely. He, of all people, had given her the comfort she needed at that crucial time, and try as she might, she could not dispel a yearning inside her to be held by those arms again.

'Stop it!' she said out loud. 'You only feel this because you are still emotionally unstable. He simply did what any human being would have done in the circumstances. It was an act of kindness, no more.'

She stood up and walked to her piano, then sat down and began to play. This must be her living and breathing for the next few days to catch up on her ten days in Devon. Anton must be put aside as a pleasant moment when their paths crossed. She was bound to meet him on plenty of occasions in the future on a professional level, and that was how she must keep it.

Norman Flaxman proved to be an excellent tutor, helping Natasha cope with the many new pieces of piano music that she had to learn over the winter months. She was very much in demand and reached the enviable position of being offered too much work from which she and Suzy could choose how to fit together a dazzling career.

She found herself travelling much more than she had ever done before, staying in hotels in cities from Bristol to Birmingham, Leeds to Liverpool, making solo performances as well as playing with all the top orchestras in the country. She was offered several recording contracts and was relieved that she had not signed exclusively with one company. Her reviews were still as good, though she almost stopped cutting them out and sticking them in her scrap book now her mother would not be there to read them. In the end, she decided to carry on cutting them out after all. It did not seem right to stop.

She contacted her brother and sister-in-law regularly, hearing the latest up-date on his thoughts for her spring holiday in Vancouver. She could not wait to see Tom again and to talk face to face with Sally whom she had not seen since their wedding five years ago.

Christmas was a time she was not looking forward to. It had always meant a trip to Devon, a quiet time relaxing, walking across the hills. This year, she would not be there. The house was still there, of course, almost as she had left it a few weeks before. She knew she had to go and sort everything out one day, but could not face that yet. As for selling the house, which had been suggested to her by several people, that was out of the question. Perhaps she could let it later on, just to keep it from becoming run down.

'You will spend Christmas with me, won't you?' Suzy had said, but Natasha had declined, making excuses of other commitments. She had heard of

Suzy's Christmases, with parties and general over-
indulgence in the food, drink and sex departments.
Suzy had never been a family girl and only ever
contacted her parents very occasionally. That was
where the two of them differed so much, and now
Natasha, who would have loved the intimacy of her
family, did not have one.

On Boxing Day the phone rang.

'I missed you at Suzy's,' the voice said. 'I felt sure we
would meet there on Christmas Eve. Where have you
been hiding?'

Natasha felt her heart lurch inside.

'Suzy's rave-ups are not really my scene, I'm afraid,'
she managed to say. 'I've spent the time on my own
this year.'

'On your own?'

'Well, I spoke to Tom yesterday. He phoned about
eight last night. Apart from the party, how did you
spend your time?'

She felt on edge and found the conversation stilted.
The time lapse since she last saw him had made them
strangers again.

'Oh, the usual family get-together at my grandmother's in Devon.'

Natasha felt tears prick the back of her eyes.

'Are you all right?'

She swallowed hard.

'Yes,' she gulped. 'I was just thinking.'

'Of course, how insensitive of me. Sorry. What I
really phoned for was to ask you if you'd like to come
out for a drink. I'm back in town now. Can you make
this evening?'

The old thoughts flooded back into her head. Would
it be wise to take up his offer, or should she plead a

previous engagement? After all, she would not be the only woman he had been taking out over the recent past. Maria, whom she had met briefly in Devon, had been his frequent partner and some said their relationship was more than casual.

Still, what harm would one little drink do? She had to admit she had been feeling lonely and more than a tiny bit sorry for herself for the last few days. This might cheer her up.

'Why not,' she replied, trying to sound as if it did not matter to her either way.

'At eight? I'll pick you up? OK?'

'OK.'

She was already regretting her decision and would have changed her mind had he not phoned off immediately. Perhaps he sensed her doubt and denied her the chance to back out. She considered calling him to cancel, but her courage failed her. No, eight o'clock it was.

For the rest of the day, she tried to practise. She sat many times at the keyboard, her hands beginning to do the work at which she was so talented, but her concentration lapsed and her playing was bad. She made herself cups of tea, a bowl of salad, a glass of wine, coffee galore, in between each attempt, but finally gave up in disgust. She could not relax.

'I might as well start getting ready to go out,' she decided at about six o'clock, knowing full well that two hours was a ridiculous amount of time to shower and change.

However, she went to her bedroom and opened the wardrobe door, taking one outfit after another, holding it up against herself in front of the mirror.

'Too dressy!'

'Too drab.'

'Too sexy!'

'Too bright.'

And so it went on. The problem was, she did not know where he was taking her for this drink. If it were a pub, then jeans and sweater would be suitable, but if they were going to one of the expensive hotels in the West End, she would need to look smart.

It was almost an hour later that she eventually made her choice of a skirt and top that could probably be worn anywhere. She raked in the bottom of the wardrobe for her navy shoes, and selected clean underwear and dark blue stockings from the drawer, laying them on the bed before going to the bathroom to shower.

She stood in the warm jets for a long time, allowing the water to stream through her hair, which reached almost to her waist with the weight of the steaming flow. Then she turned and felt the shower on her face, her neck, and her breasts which reacted to the sensation of the gentle caress of the water. She closed her eyes, imagining hands that might equal their arousal. She felt the pert nipples with her own hands as she covered her body with smooth shower gel, suddenly aware of other reactions throughout her body, showing an urgency, a need to be loved.

'Anton,' she whispered, longingly.

She turned off the shower abruptly. What the hell did she think she was doing? It was a mistake to be seeing him, there was no doubt, to be finding herself in this state. She rubbed herself hard with the towel as if in punishment at her unwanted reverie. She would have to tell him when he arrived that she just did not feel like going out.

Too true, she snorted angrily. You actually felt like staying in, you stupid fool, and not alone!

Returning to the bedroom, she swiftly dressed in her jeans and sweater, dried her hair and put on the minimum of eye make-up. She glanced at the clock. Ten minutes to eight. She paced up and down the room, trying to release the tension that had built up inside her.

The ring of the doorbell made her physically jump, so she paused a moment, taking some deep breaths, before going to answer it. It rang again. She pulled it open impatiently, a scowl spread across her forehead.

'God, what a greeting!' Anton exclaimed, a puzzled look on his face. 'What have I done to deserve this?'

He took a step forward, trying to pass Natasha and enter the flat. She stepped in front of him.

'Look,'' she said unable to meet his eyes. 'I've changed my mind. I don't think it's a good idea. I've got a bit of a headache.'

'Sorry. You'll have to do better than that.' He spoke firmly, the hint of annoyance in his voice. 'I didn't come all this way to be let down.'

He took hold of her shoulders and moved her aside, stepping into the flat. He found his own way into the lounge and sat down. Reluctantly, she closed the door and followed him, still aware of the place where his hands had gripped her. She stood just inside the room some distance from him and raised her eyes to meet his.

'Come and sit down,' he ordered, patting the seat next to him. 'What brought on this change of heart so suddenly?'

She obeyed.

'I don't know,' she lied, dropping her eyelids under

the gaze of his steely eyes. 'I feel a bit strange.' At least this was not a lie. She still felt shocked at herself.

'And when did this condition begin?'

'Just now, in the shower.'

He laughed, his head held back, hair shimmering, teeth even and pearly white, eyes a brilliant blue.

'It's not fair!' she sighed.

'What's not fair?'

How could she tell this man how she felt about him, how his presence excited her? How could she confess to her erotic day-dream, her desires for him?

'Nothing,' was all she could murmur.

'Don't you think you need snapping out of these doldrums, Tasha?' It was the first time he had used the shortened form of her name. 'You're not doing yourself any favours, are you? Come on. I insist.'

'Where were you taking me?'

'A place I often go, up west.'

'I'm not dressed for that, am I?'

She scanned his immaculate dress, the cut of his blazer accentuating his broad shoulders, the blue stripe in the shirt matching the colour of his eyes perfectly. He was shaking his head.

'I'll give you ten minutes. Is that long enough?'

She disappeared without a word, throwing off her sweater as soon as the door closed behind her.

Come on, pull yourself together, woman. He is not a wolf. He is simply making a friendly gesture to a lonely female at Christmas time.

She did not allow herself to appreciate the silky touch of the underwear as her shaking hands guided it on to her shivering body. As quickly as possible, she slipped into the skirt and top, stepping into the elegant high-heeled shoes, and sitting down at her mirror.

More carefully, she made up her face and styled her hair then stood before the long mirror to pass judgement.

'You'll do!' she grinned sarcastically at her reflection, then wiping the smile off her face, she returned to the lounge.

'Not a bad transformation in only slightly over the set time,' he joked, but his eyes told Natasha of his approval.

'You look lovely,' he whispered as he helped her on with her coat.

'Thank you. You don't look so bad yourself.'

'Friends?'

'Friends!'

She took the arm he offered and praised herself for coping so much better with her emotions.

She was glad at her choice of clothes as it happened, feeling comfortable, yet smart, fashionable, yet not high fashion in the lounge bar where they sat half an hour later.

'Kir, please,' she had replied to his question when they arrived and stood at the bar glancing round the room. They had carried their own drinks to a table in the corner beside the glowing log fire.

Now they faced each other across the small round table, Natasha chastised herself for almost ruining this chance to get to know Anton better. She found she wanted to talk to him about her mother, felt she was able to confide in him, drew comfort from his sympathetic ear.

He, in turn, spoke of his grandmother and his affection for her. The tension that had grown between them at Natasha's flat gradually melted away and she relaxed with the return of the feeling she had had before, that she had known Anton for a very long time.

'Same again?' she found herself asking as he drained his glass.

'Please,' he smiled. She felt his approving gaze as she walked to the bar and stood waiting to be served.

'I'd like a romp with you, sweetie,' whined a voice in her ear.

She turned her head slightly, blushing scarlet.

'Has anyone ever told you you've got sexy legs,' he went on.

Natasha threw a desperate look over her shoulder. Anton was still watching her, but she realized he could not possibly be aware of what this man was saying. The barman came and took her order. He turned his back on her to fetch the drinks.

'Are you with him?' The man jerked his head in the direction of Anton.

'Yes.' Anger was beginning to rise in her, as he leered drunkenly towards her.

'You must be one of his easy women. A good lay, I'll bet. You know what I'd like to do....' He leaned so close she could smell the alcohol on his breath. He continued speaking, his language becoming foul with obscenities. She felt unable to move, so repulsed was she by his words. If only the barman would hurry.

Suddenly, the man's expression changed as he was lifted off his feet and ended up hanging over the bar.

'How dare you speak like that to my friend?' boomed Anton at her side, reminding her in his anger of their earliest encounter. 'You vile example of an upper-class lecher.'

'You think you're any better than me? You're the one with all the women in tow, and you have the nerve to call me a lecher. You should tell this "friend" of yours what you're really like.'

'Come on, Tasha. Let's get away from this undesirable company. We'll finish these drinks and go.'

The barman had returned and Anton hurriedly paid him, took both glasses in one hand, steering Natasha away with the other.

'It's OK, I'm going, but I don't forget, Mr Cocksure. Don't you worry, I'll pay you back for this.'

'How do you know him?' Natasha managed to ask when she had regained her breath and her seat.

'Unfortunately, I had the pleasure of going to school with him. Would you believe it, he's the Honourable Mr Pomfret? Nothing honourable about him, and there never has been. Are you OK?'

'Yes, fine, though now I know what it must feel like to get an obscene phonecall!'

'He's just a load of hot air. Ignore everything he said.'

'I'll try,' Natasha promised.

Quite easily, she had been able to push the Honourable Mr Pomfret's obscenities to the back of her mind, but try as she might she could not help remembering his words about Anton. 'One of his easy women,' he had said, and 'a good lay', as if Anton only associated with 'good lays'.

The atmosphere of the evening failed to recover after that incident, and Natasha genuinely felt the beginnings of a headache as she finished her second Kir rather more hurriedly than the first. Neither of them spoke in the car. Natasha brooded over Pomfret's incriminating words. How true could they be? she wondered. If only she knew.

Anton seemed to have been affected more than he

would have liked to admit by this chance encounter. He stopped outside her apartment, keeping the engine running.

'Thanks, Anton,' she simply said, recognizing the hint that he would not be coming in for coffee.

'My pleasure. We must meet again soon.'

Natasha took this to be a polite way of saying the opposite, but returned his brief kiss before climbing out of the car and unlocking the door.

'Warning, gutter press in action,' was how Suzy greeted Natasha on the telephone the next Sunday morning. 'I'm on my way.'

Ten minutes later Suzy entered, armed with one of the more salacious Sunday papers. The offending article concerned the other side of the famous conductor, Anton Martineau, listing his many conquests, paramours, lovers, in explicit terms. The final paragraph mentioned a new affair with a mysterious woman with raven tresses and an hour-glass figure.

'Who is this striking bombshell?' Natasha read. 'New putty in the maestro's hands'. 'An orgy of music-making....'

'What provoked this attack?' asked Suzy when Natasha had finished.

'It must be that upper-class twit who tried to pick me up. He said he'd get even with Anton.'

Over a glass of red wine, Natasha began to confide in her friend.

'I hadn't wanted to come to your party because I couldn't face the physical side of things, if you don't mind my admitting it!'

'No, but you shouldn't have been on your own. No wonder you fell into the arms of the first offer that came along.'

'Suzy! How dare you! Surely you don't believe what you yourself called the gutter press?'

'You don't know how pleased I am to hear you say it. Of course I didn't believe it. I know you better than that. Tell me all.'

By the time she had consumed three glasses of wine Natasha felt brave enough to confess her confused mind to Suzy, even to her arousing thoughts in the shower. Suzy let her continue the whole story without interruption.

'You are in a bad way, my poor little flower,' she soothed. 'The more I think about it, the more this trip to Canada seems like a brilliant idea. You'll have so much to do and so many places to visit and people to meet, mainly men I hope, that you won't have a second to think such thoughts ever again.'

'I suppose you're right.'

'No suppose about it. I know I'm right.'

'Thanks, Suzy. You always make me see sense.'

But despite all the promises she made to Suzy and herself, there was one fact she could not wipe from her mind.

That night she tossed restlessly in her bed, sifting through everything, over and over again in her tired brain. Each time she found the logical answer to a question she asked herself, reason flew out of the window, and the same glaring truth stood plainly before her. All denials were useless. She knew only one thing was true. She wanted him, badly.

Five

The first three months of the new year proved to be hectic for Natasha, though the first concert she gave after her recent emotional turmoil produced bad reviews. These were the only such reviews she had ever had and her confidence was shaken by them.

'You have to take criticism when it's due,' Norman Flaxman told her, 'and let's face it, you haven't been quite yourself lately, have you? I've noticed a lack of commitment I don't like to see, especially in one so talented.'

Natasha had to agree about the lack of commitment, but she could not help the fear in her mind firstly that this was the beginning of the end of a shining career and secondly that the Hon Mr Pomfret had something to do with it. However, she cast these doubts to one side and achieved the usual rave reviews after her next recital.

Preparations were well underway for the Canadian trip, according to a very secretive Suzy who had obtained Tom's telephone number from Natasha and had made several trans-Atlantic calls. Natasha demanded to know what was going on many times both from her brother and her agent.

'You'll find out soon enough,' Suzy laughed in answer. 'We don't want to spoil your fun. You've got a great brother, by the way. Pity he's married!'

'I promised I'd tell you nothing, Tash. Sorry,' Tom's

voice said from the other side of the world. 'Anyway, you won't be disappointed.'

Oh, dear, Natasha mused after one of her attempts to wheedle everything out of Tom, whom she thought was more likely to give in to her persistent questions. I dread to think what they have hatched up between them. She would have to trust them, that was all.

A journey abroad, to perform in Berlin, took her mind off the impending trip. It was wonderful to share in the atmosphere of freedom and unity that still hung in the air around the city since the bringing down of the wall. She ventured through the Brandenburg Gate into what she could not believe such a short time ago had been behind the Iron Curtain. She was extremely well received by the German audiences and after her final performance a reception was held in her honour. Returning to her hotel room flushed with such acclaim, but exhausted, she threw off her shoes as soon as she had closed the door behind her and sank gratefully on to the bed.

She gazed contentedly around the room for some moments before her eyes rested on something she had not noticed when she first came in. Swinging her feet to the floor she stood up and walked quickly to the table beside the door. It was a single red rose. There was no card, no message, no name. She reached for the phone and pressed the button for reception.

'*Ja, bitte?*'

'I'm afraid I don't speak much German. It's Miss Spitzen, here. I wonder if you can help me?'

'I will try.'

'I've found a beautiful red rose here in my room with no indication of who sent it.'

'*Oh, ja, Fraulein Spitzen.* The sender wanted to

remain unknown to you. I can say no more.'

'Was it a man? Was he German, English, maybe? I'd like to thank whoever it was.'

'Sorry, my dear lady. A promise is a promise, after all.'

'Yes, I suppose so. Thanks.'

She replaced the receiver and stood the rose in a glass she found in the bathroom, putting it on the bedside table. Another enigma! Maybe she would never know and she would be sure not to ask anyone or assume anything. She had made that mistake once before and had her head bitten off in the process.

She smiled at herself in the mirror at the memory of that unfortunate incident. She had really made a fool of herself that day!

She undressed and after a swift visit to the bathroom climbed into bed. It was probably merely some kind person who had heard her playing that evening and found out where she was staying. It was as simple as that. With this confident conclusion in her mind she immediately fell asleep.

On her return to England she continued a busy period, rushing from home to Norman Flaxman's, to recording studios, to rehearsals, to concerts, with such little free time that when the telephone rang one evening when she was relaxing with a book beside the fire, she was more than a little surprised at the voice on the other end.

'Tasha, is that you?'

'Hello, Anton. How are you?'

'Busy. That's why I haven't called you.'

'Me, too. I've been all over the place, not long back from Berlin.'

'Really?'

'And you? You've been abroad too, I gather?'

'Here and there, mainly there,' he laughed.

She liked that laugh. It sent ripples of pleasure down her spine. It was infectious and she giggled.

Actually, she knew exactly where Anton had travelled. She had not been able to help herself in her curiosity as to his engagements and she had a rough idea of his itinerary for the future, too. She was fully aware that he had been all over Europe during the last month, through Italy, Switzerland, and Austria for a start. She also knew that he was due to make a tour of the Far East in March. She could not tell herself why she did it, except to return to her self admission just after Christmas, but as long as she knew his whereabouts, she found she could put him to the back of her mind and concentrate on her own career.

'Can we meet?' he was saying. 'Only this time not in town.'

'I'd like that,' she cursed herself for admitting. 'When?'

'Are you free tomorrow evening?'

'As it happens I am. I have rehearsals most of the day, but a free evening.'

'Great. It's the first complete day off I'll have had in a month.'

'What a hectic life we lead.' It was her turn to laugh. 'Where are you taking me? What shall I wear this time?'

'Do I note a hint of sarcasm in your voice? Actually, casual would be best. Wrap up warm. There's an old pub in the middle of Epping Forest where the bar food is excellent.'

'And where there'll be no prying eyes of the press, or

any old buddies of yours?'

'Tasha, I don't like that sort of thing any more than you do. In fact, I hate being labelled in such a way. If I could be at all bothered I would sue that foul gutter rag.'

'There's no smoke without fire, they say.'

'You don't have to associate with the likes of me if you feel like that. Just forget I asked you.'

'No, Anton. I didn't mean it. Tomorrow it is.'

'7.30?'

She scolded herself for her outspokenness. She had touched a nerve, to be sure. Maybe he genuinely was not the womanizer he seemed. After all, yes, he was seen in public with a variety of women, but there was no evidence these relationships ever went any further than that. She remembered his correct behaviour towards her after the French meal. If ever he had had the opportunity to flaunt his masculinity, that must have been the easiest. He had certainly been nothing but a gentleman.

The sleek silver car held the winding roads well with the light, sure touch of Anton's hands on the wheel. Natasha sat comfortably beside him watching those hands, so expressive yet strong.

He had not mentioned their telephone conversation when he picked her up on the dot of 7.30, but simply grinned and nodded approval at her jeans and sweater beneath the warm padded jacket. She had followed him to the car without a word and enjoyed feeling the power of the sports engine as they had begun their journey.

Natasha had omitted to tell Suzy of Anton's invitation and had not permitted herself a moment's deliberation about her relationship with a man whom she accepted was attractive to her. As she pulled on her boots just before Anton had arrived to fetch her she felt calm and resigned. They were 'just good friends'.

The pub was warm both in atmosphere and temperature and by the end of the evening Natasha felt sleepy and content. The food had lived up to its reputation and the place had been sufficiently full for a constant buzz of talking to provide a background noise to their own conversation.

They sauntered towards the parked car in the pitch darkness, his arm gently around her waist, her head resting against his shoulder, as if it were the most natural thing in the world. She gazed up at the stars, brilliant in comparison to the black moonless sky. He followed her gaze and they stopped, staring together upwards.

'Look, the Plough.'

'And the Pole Star.'

'I love star gazing.'

'Me, too.'

She turned to him and sensed his eyes on her in the darkness. She felt firm hands on her shoulders as he lowered his face to hers. Their lips met briefly, sending electric shocks all over her body. Then he let her go as quickly as he had held her,

'Come on,' he whispered hoarsely. 'You'll get cold.'

He reached for her hand and they walked to the car in silence. He unlocked the doors and they climbed in.

'I'm off to the Far East in a couple of weeks and I'm desperately busy until then. I might not see you until after your Canadian performances are finished.'

'And I'm staying on there to have a holiday with

Tom. Suzy's coming with me.'

'Oh,' was all he said. The engine purred into life.

'So I won't see you for nearly two months.'

'I suppose not.'

He was speaking very vaguely, and as Natasha turned to him she noticed a far-away look in his eyes. He was sounding very casual, in fact too casual. Surely he could not be regretting their enforced separation?

Too soon she recognized the flats as the car slowed to a halt outside the door. He turned off the engine and slipped his arm lightly round her shoulders. She rested her head against his, feeling the deep sigh that shook through him. Her eyes searched for his in query, but he turned away.

'Things might have been different,' he said barely audibly.

'What do you mean, Anton?'

He still kept his eyes averted, staring blankly through the windscreen and along the street.

'I wish I could....'

'Could what?'

'Nothing. One day, maybe I can make you understand.'

'Understand what? Oh, Anton, please explain. Come in. Have a coffee. What's troubling you? We can talk about it, can't we? Won't that help?'

'No, I must go now, while I can. I'll ring you before I fly out to Tokyo.'

Turning quickly towards her he caught her unawares. Cupping his hands powerfully behind her head he searched for her lips with his. Instead of returning a brief kiss as before, Natasha found herself reeling under the force of his mouth, sensual and open, his tongue penetrating her parted lips. Alive with desire she answered with her lips, her tongue, her arm reaching out to hold him in the confined space of the car.

'Go,' he cried suddenly, gasping for breath. 'Please go now.'

Natasha found herself propelled from the car staggering shakily towards the outer door. Her hands would not function properly and the car had long gone before the key had been inserted in the lock. Reaching the sanctity of her own flat at last, she threw herself into a chair, breathing deeply.

Natasha heaved a sigh of relief as the jet became airborne. To her, take-off was always the worst part of the flight. She uncrossed her fingers, opened her eyes and smiled at Suzy.

'If you could see your face,' Suzy laughed, 'you superstitious old thing. Crossing fingers!'

'I just don't like take-off, that's all. I'm OK now.'

'I'm too excited to be scared. I've been looking forward to this trip for so long. You realize it was almost six months ago that it was first put to me for you to play in Canada?'

'I know. It's been an unbelievable six months too. So much has happened.'

Suzy began chatting to the man next to her, leaving Natasha with her thoughts.

I've grown up these past months, with Mum dying in the midst of my success.

She had still continued her scrapbook, even inserting the bad reviews in the New Year. She had also found herself scouring the arts pages of all the daily newspapers for references to Anton and cutting them out, sticking those in beside hers.

She had heard only once from him since his strange yet passionate outburst at the end of their pub visit. As he had promised he phoned her the day before he was due to leave for Tokyo. He was cool, embarrassed perhaps, and neither of them said much, though he did repeat the phrase he had said before, 'One day I'll make you understand', though what was behind this she really could not imagine.

She had disciplined herself as she had managed to do before to practise and perform with determination and total involvement and the time of her departure to Canada sped nearer.

Tom and Suzy had maintained their secrecy over their plans, which caused them great amusement through many phone calls. Natasha had even appealed to Sally on one occasion, but Tom had primed his wife and she gave nothing away. One tiny clue had escaped Tom's lips, however, and that was a passing reference to Natasha's birthday towards the end of April. She would finish her concert performances three days before that day. Perhaps they had something planned for then, she guessed, but hoped it was nothing too outrageous.

The plane made its descent to Toronto airport after a seven-hour flight.

'Thank God for a break. I could do with a breath of fresh air.'

'I need to stretch my legs. Actually, I find flying boring after the terrifying take-off.'

'I haven't been bored at all. I've been chatting to a really smashing bloke.'

'So I noticed, Suzy. See anything in trousers and you go for him.'

'Anything's better than being an old misery. You ought to find yourself a man, Tasha. The world's full of them, all looking out for attractive females like you.'

'So you keep telling me. I'm quite happy as I am, thank you very much.'

'Not for much longer, if what Tom tells me is true.'

'Suzy, if he's trying the art of match-making, I'll never forgive either of you.'

The flight to Vancouver seemed endless, but at last the pilot announced the approach. Touchdown was smooth and there was Tom to meet them. A taxi whisked them through the outskirts of the city to his flat where a welcome meal awaited them.

The hotel was comfortable enough, though impersonal.

'I'm glad I'm not here on my own,' Natasha told her friend. 'These places can be so lonely.'

Later, she felt like eating her words after Suzy had insisted on going down to the bar where they were approached by two young men whom Natasha assumed fancied their chances. Suzy seemed to be giving them every encouragement and if Natasha had not pleaded exhaustion she dreaded to think where it might have ended.

'I'm not a prude,' she insisted after her friend had finished moaning at her in the sanctuary of their room, 'but we don't seem to have even the slightest resemblance to each other in our outlook.'

'Another time, I'll go down to the bar on my own.'

'No, don't be silly. I'll come with you. I like men, but I'm not prepared to be picked up by any Tom, Dick or Harry who happens along.'

'OK, you win. I'll behave myself next time.'

As it was, Suzy found herself alone quite a lot while Natasha attended rehearsals. Natasha found the Canadians warm and generous in their reception of her and she was introduced to so many new people her head was in a spin. Both women were escorted round the city on a sight-seeing tour. Natasha fell in love with the place, which was coming alive now after the long, severe winter.

The days of the concerts came and went, with Tom and Sally as her greatest fans.

'Sis, you're a genius,' Tom exclaimed after a dazzling performance of Beethoven's Emperor Concerto. 'Do you realize I've not heard you play live since we emigrated – though I have bought all your albums. A friend of mine sends them out to me on release.'

They were back at Tom and Sally's flat. Natasha beamed at Tom. She had not realized that he took such an interest in her career. Then she laughed as Tom took on the guise of an interviewer, an imaginary microphone held between them.

'Tell me, Miss Spitzen, to whom do you attribute this meteoric rise to stardom?'

'Well, apart from myself, of course,' she began in a sweet, Southern drawl not unlike Marilyn Monroe, 'I'd like to thank my first teacher, Miss Western, not forgetting my parents and my dear brother, Tom.'

'And later, Miss Spitzen?'

'Why, yes. We mustn't forget dear Piers and later on, Norman Flaxman, who has become my mentor.'

Natasha had entered into the spirit of her brother's prank, acting the part well.

'Go on, Miss Spitzen. Tell us more.'

'Well, of course, as I have said many, many times before, where would I be without the undying loyalty of my companion, friend and agent, Ms Suzy Dannovitch?'

There was loud applause at her side and Natasha turned to see Suzy grinning from ear to ear beside her.

'Oh, please don't stop here, Miss Spitzen. Tell us more.'

Natasha curtsied extravagantly.

'That's all, I'm afraid.'

'Oh, surely not, Miss Spitzen. Surely you can think of someone else, someone who has had an influence on your playing, someone who has become increasingly important to you over the past nine months.'

'That's not cricket.' Natasha had returned to her normal voice. She faced her brother, hands on hips, a confused look on her face.

'OK. A fair cop!'

Later, when they were alone, Tom brought up the subject of Anton again, in a straightforward manner this time.

'I only asked because I couldn't help noticing the look in your eyes when I was over in England. Mum had already commented on it in her letter, as I told you.'

'He was incredibly kind at that time, surely you must realize that.'

'Yes, but since then. You've been out with him, haven't you?'

'What's Suzy been saying?'

'Nothing, nothing, calm down, sweet sister. Only that she's had to talk you out of deep emotional turmoil on more than one occasion. Can't you tell me? I promise I won't breathe a word to anyone.'

'Not even Sally? And especially Suzy?'

'Cross my heart.'

'It's true, I'm afraid. I love him. I have difficulty at times getting him out of my brain. I make myself practise harder and harder to rid myself.'

'But why? Not still remembering that Pete bloke, are you? That was years ago. You've recovered.'

'No, not that. It's Anton. He feels very little for me, at least that's how it seems. I've only been out with him a couple of times and he's always been the perfect gentleman, despite the reputation he has in certain sections of Fleet Street.'

'I heard about that, too. Do you feel you can tell me?'

Relieved to have an outlet at last for her troubles, Natasha related to Tom every detail of her meetings with Anton, beginning with the tempestuous concerto and ending with his passionate kiss.

'What can he have meant? He almost seemed to want more, yet something held him back. It wasn't fear, but some regret. I just couldn't understand. So I've forced myself not to think of him too much. It hurts, but it's the only way I can deal with it.'

'Poor Tash. I honestly didn't realize you'd got it so bad or I wouldn't have teased you in our mock interview.'

'Forgiven, and thanks.'

'When will you see him again?'

'Who knows. This year, next year, sometime, never. You probably know the answer to that better than I do.'

'I suppose I probably do. Come on, let's join the others.'

The official side of Natasha's visit was soon over and after the reception held in the largest banqueting hall Natasha could have ever imagined, she was free to

enjoy the next two weeks in Vancouver. The weather
had taken a turn for the better and the second half of
April was forecast warm and dry.

Preparations were under way for their holiday in
Tom's cottage on Vancouver Island and Natasha felt
at last able to share Suzy's excitement. Something
had been planned for her birthday on the 23rd, she
could tell, but what that was she had not a clue.

They arrived in a small motor craft that belonged to
Tom and Sally and which had been moored in dry dock
in a large marina for the winter. The first day was
taken up with spring-cleaning the cottage, which
Suzy claimed belied its title.

'Cottage, you call it? More like a mansion!'

It was a single-storeyed wooden building with four
official bedrooms and many camp beds and put-you-
ups tucked into corners of every room.

'We always invite so many people to stay,' Sally told
her. 'It's great fun, you'll see. I think it's about time
Natasha knew at least some of her surprise, don't
you?'

'Yes, please. I would like to know!'

'Well, it's a party, here at the cottage, with lots of
our friends.'

Natasha sighed with relief. That was all, a party for
her birthday. Well, she didn't mind that! To think she
had worried so much about awful things they might
be plotting. She willingly joined in the preparing of
the food and travelled back to the mainland with Tom
for provisions they had forgotten.

A few brave people had ventured out in their yachts,
the first of the year.

'I don't fancy that yet. If they capsize they'll freeze.

That water's icy.'

Natasha let her hand drift in the wake of the boat, but only for a moment.

'You're right. I suppose this boat's waterproof?'

They returned to the island as sunset approached and they watched the changing colours of the sky, fiery against the silhouetted pine trees.

'It's idyllic here, Tom. No wonder you've stayed. So romantic.'

'I hope so,' Tom laughed, as they reached the jetty. 'Early night for you tonight, my girl. Big day tomorrow.'

She slept well, using the unaccustomed fresh air as her excuse. The morning was clear and bright and they braved the chill in favour of breakfast alfresco. They each gave Natasha their presents.

'There's more later,' promised Tom with a knowing look at his wife.

'When do you expect the guests to start arriving?' Suzy asked hurriedly.

'Before lunch, I hope. Then some will go home before dark, and the rest will stay.'

They finished breakfast and spent the next few hours rushing round completing the preparations. At about noon a motor boat could be seen approaching the island and the first of the guests, all local Canadian friends of Tom and Sally, arrived. For the next hour there was a steady stream of arrivals, all of whom seemed to know it was Natasha's birthday and many of whom had been to one or more of her concerts. She became very much the centre of attention and realized with amusement that she had more male admirers than Suzy, for once!

The day, as promised, proved warm and sunny,

enabling everyone to stay outside most of the time. Trestle tables had been erected on the patio at the front of the cottage and there was no shortage of chairs for those who wanted them, or food for lunch, or drink. As each new arrival set foot on the wooden jetty there were introductions and greetings and toasts to the guest of honour.

'You look lovely, Sis, if a brother is allowed to say such things these days.'

'Thanks, Tom. You've made my day.'

'Not yet, I haven't.'

'What do you mean? Not more tricks up your sleeve?'

At that moment a different sound could be heard above the noise of chatter and laughter. Everyone turned to watch as a single-engined plane approached coming lower all the time. The party became quiet.

'It's getting too low,' whispered Natasha. 'The pilot had better watch out. It'll hit the water.'

'It's OK, Sis. He knows what he's doing. He's got floats instead of wheels.'

She had not noticed that. 'He's landing on the water.'

Tom nodded.

'Is he coming here, to the party?'

Tom nodded again.

'Who is it?'

'He's a colleague of mine – owns a quarter-share in the plane, lucky bloke. He's bringing a few other people. It seats twelve.'

Natasha watched fascinated as the little plane landed smoothly on the water, then taxied round to make the final run in. A large area of the jetty had been cleared of boats for it to moor and the crowd waited patiently for the pilot to bring it in.

At last, the engine stopped and the propellers were still. A door at the side opened and young men and women began to climb down. Natasha had stood in the same place the whole time and was suddenly aware that not only Tom, but Sally and Suzy and a good few others had joined her. Why were they all so interested in her, she wondered as she felt many eyes on her face?

Then she knew. When she thought the last passenger had alighted from the plane, she realized there was one last man, a man she thought looked familiar. His blond head was bent as he stooped to pass through the door and in that moment she recognized him.

Anton! What was he doing here? Did he know she was here too? Or, worst of all, was it planned?

Then she knew it was; it had been all along. What a dirty trick to play on someone as a birthday surprise. How could they? How could he deceive her, not tell her? And yet what was it he had said? Something about not seeing her until her Canadian performances were over? He had seemed too casual, too vague. Yes, he must have been in on the secret from the beginning. She would show them what she thought of the whole idea.

Before Anton's feet had even reach the jetty, Natasha had stormed briskly away. Before anyone could stop her she had entered the cottage and slammed the door, and finding her bedroom, locked herself in.

Six

'Go away, you Judas!' Natasha cried after Tom's third attempt to persuade her to open the door. 'You betrayed me.'

'No, Tash. It wasn't like that.'

'I told you everything in confidence.'

'I know, and I kept it all to myself. I needed to know how you felt, partly out of my concern for you, but partly to be sure you'd want him to come here.'

'But I didn't!'

'We arranged it ages ago, Sis.'

'But if only he'd said. He deceived me, too.'

'Open the door, please, Tash. It'll be easier to explain.'

'Are you alone?'

'Yes. The others have gone back to the party.'

Reluctantly, Natasha turned the key in the lock. The face she presented to Tom was stormy, but not tear-stained. She had determined not to cry. Her mother had always told her it was unlucky to cry on your birthday, so she had bitten her lip hard and forbidden tears to come. She let Tom into the room and relocked the door . They sat side by side on the bed.

'I'm sorry our brilliant idea misfired, honestly I am, but we didn't really invite him here as your lover, just as a friend. He doesn't even know it's your birthday. I simply invited him here to the party when I learned

95

he was flying home this way from the Far East tour. That's all.'

'He called me Miss Spitfire once, you know. I suppose I deserve that name again. What must everyone think?'

'Don't worry about everyone else. I mumbled something about your having a headache when you woke up this morning. A couple of pills and a quiet few minutes rest can do wonders for a bad head.'

Natasha hugged her brother.

'I feel better already.'

The party was in full swing when they returned and Natasha was greeted by several well-wishers who enquired after her headache. She smiled in return.

'Much better, thanks.'

Suzy approached, looking rather sheepish.

'I could do murder sometimes, I really could,' Natasha murmured close to her ear, 'but I forgive you.'

'Glad you're feeling better, Tash. No offence meant.'

'Or taken.'

Natasha spent the following hour circulating among the guests. Tom had already introduced her to many whose names she had forgotten, but it did not matter. They were all extremely friendly and she found herself chattering easily to them. Out of the corner of her eye she caught glimpses of Anton, but they succeeded in avoiding each other quite well. Sooner or later, Natasha knew she would have to speak to him, but managed to put off that moment for as long as possible.

She was at the table replenishing her glass with fruit punch when she sensed him behind her. He had not touched her or spoken, but she knew it was him.

She turned slowly and looked up at him.

'Hello,' she said, unable to hold his gaze.

'Are you OK? You did a disappearing act just as I arrived. Have you that much of an aversion to me?'

She did not, could not reply. They walked together through the crowded patio in front of the cottage.

'Thank you for coming.' It sounded so wet, but she could think of nothing else to say.

'Shall we go for a walk? I haven't seen anything at all of this island, have you?'

'I haven't. We've been so busy since we arrived getting everything ready for this do.'

He took her glass and put it with his on a shelf just inside the cottage door. Then they turned the corner round the side of the cottage.

'Which way?'

She shrugged. She did not mind.

They walked along beside the water, watching the boats weaving about amongst each other. There were not many, so early in the year, but they looked attractive against the hazy blue of the spring sky. Natasha could see the tower blocks of the city in the distance and stood still for a moment to try and identify the flats where Tom lived. Anton stopped and stared across the water beside her.

'Are you sorry I came?' he asked abruptly.

She looked up at his face unable, not for the first time, to understand the message in his eyes. She began walking again and he caught up with her.

'No, of course not.'

'Only I saw the expression on your face as I left the plane. It reminded me of that first rehearsal we had together. Do you remember?'

'Miss Spitfire, you mean?' She laughed and felt

some of the tension drain from her. 'I was annoyed at my brother and Suzy for inviting you, but they've tried to explain.'

It was Anton's turn to remain silent.

'I've spent the past weeks trying to push you right out of my mind and I'd just about started to relax, when you turned up.'

'Gee, thanks.'

'I didn't mean that I don't like your company. I do, very much, and I thoroughly enjoyed going out with you those few times.'

'What then?'

His voice sounded so strange she halted again and turned to him.

'Don't you know? Haven't you an inkling of the effect you've had on me?'

He waited for her to continue. Careful, Tasha, she checked herself, don't say anything you'll regret.

'It was the last time, mainly, although I can't say I hadn't already found you very attractive before that.'

'Was it something I said?'

'Well, yes. You remember? In your car, when you dropped me at my apartment? You were so mysterious? You said some very odd things like wishing things could be different and maybe one day you'd make me understand.'

'Do you remember anything else that happened then, in the car?'

He had gently placed his hands on her shoulders and bent his head so their foreheads almost touched. His piercing blue eyes held hers hypnotically. Natasha felt the hot needles of a blush spread up to her face, but she could not avert her gaze.

'You kissed me,' she whispered shyly.

'But I'd kissed you before, twice.'

'I know. Don't imagine I could have forgotten.'

She knew he was teasing her and loved it. She would play along with his game for as long as he wanted.

'So why mention it? Was it in any way different to the other two?'

'Mmm,' she sighed, memories returning.

'How was it different?'

'It was longer, firmer, more demanding.'

'Arousing?'

'Mmm.' Please, don't stop, she thought.

'Making you want more?'

'Mmm.' Yes, as many as you like, her swirling brain answered.

'Was it in any way like this?'

Natasha closed her eyes as his hand cupped her head, pulling her to him. Instinctively, her arms wrapped round his neck as his parted lips found hers. The kiss began gently as he nibbled and teased her soft, receptive mouth, gradually becoming more forceful as his sensual lips were answered with equal arousal in her. His tongue probed the inside of her mouth, stirring a deep need in her.

They paused for breath, her face nuzzled into his neck, which she kissed tenderly.

'There was some similarity,' she whispered, 'but I think another reminder would help jog my memory a little....'

The end of her sentence was curtailed by Anton's mouth returning to hers and for a long time they were lost in a kiss so powerful, Natasha could not believe it possible. She had been kissed many times before, but never with such intensity. Nor had she ever experienced the yearning for the sexual fulfilment she craved now.

'Tasha!'

The voice startled her, brought her back to earth with a jolt.

'Tasha! Anton! Are you there?'

It was Tom, out searching for them.

'We're over here,' Anton called, recovering slightly quicker than Natasha. 'We're on our way back.'

Tom greeted them with a wave and came to join them.

'Some of our friends are just going. It's not long to sunset.'

Neither of the other two had noticed the lengthening shadows or the chill in the air.

'I'd like to see them off,' Natasha managed to say in a voice as shaky as her legs, as she walked beside Tom. Anton followed a few strides behind. Tom spoke quietly to Natasha, a twinkle in his eyes.

'What have you been up to? You're very flushed, Sis; what some people might call looking radiant.'

She flashed him a smile.

'My birthday's turning out even better than expected, thanks to you.'

'Nothing to do with me. I wasn't there. It takes two.....'

They had almost reached the cottage and could hear the noise of laughter and music and voices beginning their farewells.

'Where've you been, birthday girl?' asked one young man. 'Fancy disappearing like that from your own party, just when I thought I was in with a chance!'

Everyone laughed.

'Birthday girl?' asked Anton.

'Yes, didn't you know?' shouted another guest as she jumped aboard the boat. 'You must have been the only one who didn't.'

'I didn't know it was your party,' Anton said quietly in her ear. 'Now I understand a bit more of your embarrassment at my arrival.'

'We were both had,' she laughed.

'But I didn't bring you a present.'

'Yes you did.'

She reached up and kissed him on the cheek.

'Now then, you two. Break it up,' interrupted Sally.

Natasha blushed and grinned at her sister-in-law. At that moment the propellers of the plane began to turn as the pilot started the engine. She turned in horror to Anton.

'You're not going yet?'

'No. I've been invited to stay.'

Natasha heaved a sigh of relief. The prospect of him departing from her life again so abruptly would only knock her back into the doldrums she had fought so hard to leave behind. They needed some time together, she knew that. Suzy and Tom had been right all along, she hated to admit it.

They stood and watched the plane taxi along the stretch of water that divided the island from the mainland, then it picked up speed, lifted off and was soon a small speck in the deepening sky. Boats were leaving too. Some people had children to go home to, others had to go to work in the morning.

Finally, all the guests who were not staying the night had made their farewells and left. Natasha had made many promises to visit or to write or to make them welcome when they came over to the UK. About a dozen were left standing in the half light watching the last boat disappear into the distance.

As on the previous evening the sky had become a beautiful mixture of brilliant colours. Tom turned to his sister before making his way back to the cottage.

'How did you describe this sky last night?'

'Romantic.'

'And do you now understand my answer?'

'You said, "I hope so", didn't you? Yes, now I understand.'

Soon there were only two people standing together watching the sky's shades darken into night. His arm rested across her shoulders, hers round his waist.

'I'm glad you're not going yet. How long before you must leave?'

'I'm due in Los Angeles in three days. We must make the most of the short while we've got.'

'And there's no time to lose!'

They both seemed to have forgotten the ten or so witnesses who were seated on the patio by the cottage, lost as they were in each other. Natasha certainly would not have cared had she realized they were there. She was feeling the most buoyant she had ever felt in her life. She did not even notice the darkness descending about them until Tom called them away from the water's edge.

'You'll fall in if you don't look what you're doing,' he laughed. 'Come on, come and join the party. We don't allow the guest of honour to be absent for too long.'

Natasha shivered as the evening chill penetrated her clothing. They found their way back to the others.

'Shall we go inside?' suggested Sally.

The oil lamps had been lit and the cottage glowed with a welcoming warmth. Supper was laid out in the kitchen. Natasha discovered she was ravenous, wondering if it was the fresh air that had caused it!

'It's a wonder you've got room for anything else,' teased Suzy, when at last they had a moment to themselves. 'I thought you'd eaten enough of him!'

Natasha grinned happily at her friend.

'I forgive you for that remark. Just think, Suzy, after all those times you tried so desperately to knock him out of my silly head, it turns out he fancies me, too.'

'More than fancies, I should think. You're both as daft as the other.'

'Jealous!'

'Maybe you're right. There's many a girl would give a small fortune to be in your shoes at this moment.'

Natasha said nothing. A dark cloud had suddenly passed over her at Suzy's remark. It was a certainty that Anton was popular with the ladies. Surely, she was not just a statistic in his love life. Surely, his demonstration of affection was not merely turned on at the flick of any switch. Surely, she meant more to him than that.

'Hey, snap out of it. I didn't mean anything, you idiot. I can tell how he feels about you by the look in those gorgeous eyes of his.'

'Sorry. I'm silly, that's all.'

Suzy disappeared from her side, swept away by David, a friend of Tom's, leaving Natasha deep in her disturbing thoughts. Hadn't there been something that Anton had wanted to confide in her in the car back in England? Hadn't he been trying to tell her of some sort of problem? She went over his words again in her mind. It was as if there was a barrier that existed between them then. One day he hoped she'd understand – but what? Did it still exist now, she

wondered with dread and if so what was it? He had
certainly covered it up well this evening, that was for
sure.

Well, she would have to do the same. He would tell
her when he was ready, if there was anything to tell,
that is. Meanwhile, she must put all such thoughts
aside and enjoy herself.

A discussion of the following day's events broke into
her subconscious and she joined the group of people
around her brother. She would fit in with any arrangements he chose to make for the remainder of her
holiday.

She caught sight of Suzy on the sofa, making a
meal, as her friend would so aptly have put it, of
David. Suzy really had the knack of deriving as much
pleasure from a man in as short a space of time as
Natasha had ever seen. Then she could forget him just
as quickly.

If only I could be like that, she wished. If only I could
share her lack of inhibitions, her love of life, her devil-
may-care attitude towards men.

She doesn't get hurt, in fact she doesn't give a damn.
Look at her now, not a care in the world, probably with
the bedroom as the next step from here. She makes it
all look so easy.

With the determination that she would try and take
a few leaves out of Suzy's book, Natasha found Anton.
No, she was not fast and loose like her friend, but she
would make an effort to relax, to take each day as it
came, each stage as it happened, without always
reverting to doubt and negative thoughts.

'You're quiet,' Anton remarked.

'Tired, I guess. After all, I've had an exciting day!'

'Can you take a little more excitement?'

She responded warmly to his kiss.

The size of the cottage restricted sleeping arrangements to the extent that Suzy was disappointed, if her intentions were what Natasha had guessed. At Tom's instigation, they were all divided into the two sexes, even the married couples, and slept in dormitories of several people in each room.

'Robben b...' whispered Suzy.

Natasha grinned to herself in the darkness.

'Don't be greedy,' she answered almost inaudibly, a giggle trying to surface. 'Save some of him till tomorrow!'

The morning dawned fine as it had on the previous day. Thinking how fortunate they were, they determined there was not a moment to be lost and after hastily preparing a picnic, they all set off to walk round the island. They had agreed they would walk as far as their energy allowed and stop at suitable intervals for refreshment.

Natasha felt exhilarated, her cheeks flushed with the cool morning air, the exertion of their brisk walk, and the company she kept. Anton grasped her hand firmly in his as if he would never let go and she remembered their parting kisses of the night before. This was surely turning into the blissful dream she had always wished for.

It was lunchtime when they stopped at a beach on the island coast to picnic. The warm sun allowed them all to shed a layer or two of clothing, though the water was icy, so early in the year.

'Let's try and get off on our own later,' Anton said close to her ear. She nodded, shimmers of excitement running through her.

'I'd like to see Victoria, wouldn't you?' he asked. 'It

can't be far and there are buses, I expect. It's supposed
to be very English.'

'I don't know the first thing about it,' she admitted,
'but I'm game.'

Persuading Tom and the rest of the party proved no
difficulty and at last Natasha found herself alone with
the man she loved. Anton had been right, it was not
far to Victoria and the bus which came along after a
short wait took only a few minutes to reach the
southern tip of Vancouver Island. They alighted in
the centre of the town and the first thing that caught
Natasha's eye was the red London Transport double-
decker bus.

'Home from home,' she laughed, and did not com-
plain at Anton's suggestion of a tour of the city on the
top deck. Nestled in his arms, Natasha took in only a
fraction of the sights of Victoria. It did not matter
where in the world they were at that moment as long
as she could be held in his arms. She could feel his firm
body in contact with hers, becoming aroused at his
touch. Then she knew she wanted the intimacy of
closer contact and felt frustrated at the other people
around. They had wanted to be alone together, yet
here they were surrounded by hundreds of other
tourists.

'Tomorrow we really do get away from it all,' he
promised over the tea-table in an exquisitely English
Tea Room.

'You must have read my mind. It's a lovely city, but
I'm not in the right frame of mind for sightseeing.'

They found some solitude in a beautiful garden,
where winding paths lost themselves amid profuse
green shrubs. They chose a spot furthest from the
entrance of the garden and hand in hand, like two

guilty children tiptoed into a secluded area of grass between two of the thickest hedges. Their coats laid on the ground provided protection from the damp.

Lying in his arms a few moments later, Natasha let out a deep sigh of contentment. He stroked her hair gently, running his long fingers through the dark waves. She looked into his eyes which had become a deep, deep blue.

'I do believe, Miss Spitzen,' he taunted, nibbling her ear provocatively, 'that we may have the makings of a passionate woman beneath this shy exterior.'

'Do you think so, Mr Martineau?' she responded, realizing the truth of his words as she spoke.

'I've seen evidence in your playing, Miss Spitzen, which I must confess, stimulated me to thoughts of desire.'

Natasha pulled away from him slightly, to try to read his expression. Was he taking the Mickey? Or was this his way of telling her that he had wanted her for some time? The kiss that followed left her in no doubt that it was the latter, as Natasha found herself helpless to the strength and intensity of his feelings, and they both found themselves gasping for breath minutes later.

'We're like a couple of kids,' he whispered hoarsely, 'creeping away to the park like this.'

'I know,' she answered happily. 'And I don't care.'

Amazed at herself as she was, her inhibitions had gone, leaving her the contentment of enjoying the present. Now was the important time. The future was another matter. It could look after itself when it came. She would savour the moment.

'Tasha?'

She shivered with pleasure at the sound of her own name. It was the way he said it.

'Yes?'

'I hate to say this, but *tempus fugit*. I don't know what time the buses go back, but the sun's going down already. It'll be dark soon.'

What was it about this man that made her lose all sense of time or place? She glanced at her watch. He was right, of course.

'We don't want to be stranded here, do we?' he was saying.

She gazed intently into his eyes. Don't we? There was nothing she would have liked more. He understood the message in her eyes.

'We could be stranded here if we choose.'

'What are you suggesting, Mr Martineau?'

'We could find a little hotel somewhere. The others would understand. Your brother wouldn't mind, would he?'

They lay in each other's arms in silence, eyes closed. Natasha pictured herself in a large soft bed waiting for Anton to join her. She imagined his naked body, muscular and firm, drawing ever closer to hers. She wanted him.

She opened her eyes, brought abruptly back to reality. It didn't happen like that. Of course her brother would worry. She was here in Canada as his guest, after all, and she should not really abuse that.

'It was a wonderful idea,' he admitted, 'but not to be, just yet.'

He must have had similar visions, the same arrival at reality.

'I need you, Tasha, like I've needed nobody before.'

'We were just about to send out the search party. Where have you been?'

They hung their heads in mock shame.

'Our watches stopped,' Natasha joked and her brother's features erupted in laughter.

'I haven't heard that since I said it myself, must be twenty years ago. Where were you, though?'

When they had completed the story of their afternoon, with slight omissions, over supper in the cottage, they parted for the night.

'How about a trip out in your brother's boat tomorrow – just the two of us?'

'Sounds great!'

Natasha drifted to bed, thinking of the morrow.

'Come on, Tash,' whispered Suzy from somewhere close to her in the dark. 'Tell all.'

'We did.'

'That was only half the story. I bet there was more to it than that!'

'You looked as if you were too busy making your own conquests to notice mine. But actually, now you're asking, yes it was rather special.'

'Special? What in heaven's name does that mean?'

'It means I'm madly in love with a certain handsome, blue-eyed male not a million miles from here and I don't care who knows it. It also means I think he loves me.'

'Go on. What happened?'

'Suzy, I'm tired. I'll tell you all tomorrow.'

However much Suzy tried cajoling Natasha into revealing the developments that had occurred between Anton and herself, she remained silent and eventually she slept, waking with a feeling of excitement in her stomach which she could not initially identify.

The boat trip, of course.

She wondered if Anton had arranged it with Tom yet. She was sure Tom would agree, unless he had use for the boat himself. Her first glance at Anton told her everything was all right. He merely nodded and smiled an enigmatic smile, that Natasha felt confident she was beginning to be able to interpret.

She took a leisurely shower, evoking all those previously dormant senses, as the water played with her body. She viewed herself critically in the full-length mirror – the generous, yet firm breasts, the slim waist curving out into her hips, and long slender legs. Not bad, considering she used to hate herself for being overweight.

She brushed her hair until it shone with raven highlights. She felt her hair had always been her one asset, when all else had disappointed her. She finished her make-up quickly. There was no point in wearing much face paint when you're going out in a boat.

'Ready?' Anton asked after breakfast taken again on the patio.

'Ready and willing, sir,' she smiled up at him.

'Are you sure I can trust you in his hands alone out there on the water, Tash?' called Suzy as they reached the jetty and clambered on board.

Natasha waved in reply. She could not think of an appropriate verbal answer. What she was thinking was – can I trust myself?

Seven

For a while Anton took the boat out into the waters that separate Vancouver Island from the mainland, then he swung due north, steering towards the northern tip of the island, into more open water. They had brought a cool-bag containing a bottle of white wine and a few other refreshments, anticipating being out for quite a while.

Leaving Anton outside at the wheel, Natasha explored the cabin, finding some fishing tackle tucked neatly away under the benches.

'Do you think we could fish?' she called, waving a reel and some line at him through the window. She rejoined him on deck.

'I don't know what the position is about fishing here. At home in the inland waters it's the closed season at the moment, to allow the fish to spawn and the young to grow to a decent size before being caught, poor blighters. Perhaps we'd better not, just in case.'

She returned to the cabin. There was a table with a bench either side, a galley with the usual basic equipment, and a toilet. Tom had mentioned he had slept on board occasionally in summer, but she could find no sign of a bedroom, or even a bed. He must have slept on a bench, she decided.

She returned to keep Anton company on deck. The wind was chill as the sun was still quite low in the sky, but Anton wrapped one arm around her shoulders.

She snuggled into the warmth of his body, content. They reached an isolated spot on the mainland side of the water, and Anton moored the boat a short way from the shore, letting drop the anchor.

'Wine, Madame? I thought a drop of Muscadet might please?'

He drew the cork with ease and produced two glasses from the bag. Sally had thought of everything! Natasha watched him pour the wine, clear as crystal in the now bright sunlight, and they stood on deck watching the wildlife indigenous to that coastline. She felt the refreshing cool of the Muscadet and remembered the last time they had drunk that wine together in the French restaurant in London. It seemed such a long time ago.

'You like the boat?' Anton asked after an endless silence that held them together.

She shrugged and smiled.

'It's OK, I suppose. One boat's much the same as another, isn't it?'

'Don't let Tom hear you say that. It's his pride and joy.'

'I didn't really mean that,' she laughed, then more seriously, 'I just feel happy at being here with you.'

He kissed her lips softly, so gently her knees almost gave way from under her. He took her glass and put it down with his on the side of the deck, wrapping his arms tightly round her in a bear hug.

'You're shivering. Still cold? Come on, it'll be warmer in the cabin.'

She allowed herself to be led into the cramped room below, her hand engulfed by his. She felt overwhelmed by his presence in the confined space, nervous now with anticipation. She watched as he lifted the table with ease, slotting it between the bench seats, moving the cushions together in the centre. He sat down and patted the space beside him.

So that's where Tom had slept, on a makeshift bed, and now she was being invited to join Anton on it. Gingerly, she sat down next to him, her legs swinging over the side, her hands tucked underneath her thighs, her head bent forward, her face flushed deep scarlet. She dare not look up at him knowing his eyes were on her.

What has he in mind? she asked herself, panic rising in her throat. Here I sit, having given him every encouragement, waiting for him to make the next move.

She felt his hand lightly begin to stroke her hair from her crown, down the nape of her neck and her back to her waist. His hand retraced its path over and over again, becoming firmer each time. She found she could gradually relax, the tension draining out of her body. He sensed this, too, leaving his hand on her waist a little longer, letting it drift a little lower as he succeeded in calming her.

'Tasha,' he whispered so close to her she could feel his breath on her ear. She tingled with pleasure. It was definitely the way he said it.

She smiled to herself, still keeping her face averted, afraid of her own emotions. She wanted him, she did not deny, but was she ready? Did she love him enough to give her all to this man whom, after all, she had only known for a comparatively short period?

What concerned her even more was the uncertainty of his motives. That he was fond of her, she had no doubt. That he wanted her was blatantly obvious. But could she trust him? Was she just one of many women he had won over? Did he live up to that reputation offered by Pomfret? Would he merely use her and discard her? She couldn't stand that!

'What is it, Tasha?' he was saying, his voice appealing.

His hand was still, resting on her waist, burning into her skin. She moved fractionally towards him, turning at last to meet his eyes, their piercing blue expression melting her resolve. She had known it would, but could not prevent herself from looking at him. She closed her eyes as his mouth captured hers in a most sensuous kiss, her hands reaching out to touch him, to draw him nearer.

'Don't believe idle gossip,' he said, their lips barely apart. 'I'm not a Casanova, despite my undeserved reputation.'

They moved further on to the bed, and lay side by side, her head resting on his shoulder, his arms around her. He kissed her with such intensity as if to convince her of the truth of his promise. He resumed stroking her hair, running his long fingers through the dark waves as he had done in the park.

She sighed. If this was love, then she was all for it. She studied the fine lines of his face, touching his full firm lips with the tip of her forefinger. He let her tease him for a while before nipping her finger playfully.

He let his hand follow the line of her back, into the hollow of her slim waist, over the curve of her hip. She inhaled abruptly as he cupped her breast which reacted instantly, its nipple becoming firm with her arousal. She drew his body closer to her, feeling the hardening of his sexual desire against her.

'Darling,' he whispered. 'I need you.'

Surely she was not making a mistake? Her need

persuaded her, but even if she was, she must emulate
Suzy's attitude for once and live for the present.

Anton's hand began performing magic with her
body, thrill after thrill passing through her as his deft
fingers explored. Hungrily, their lips met in a mixture
of arousal and demand, until Natasha knew for absolute certain that she craved satisfaction. She wanted
him to enter her, to bring her to fulfilment.

She did not feel the cold any more as she knelt above
him, each removing the other's clothing, until they
wore nothing but their scant undergarments. His
hand reached to unfasten her bra, lowering her breasts
to within a few inches of his face. His mouth closed on
first one then the other nipple, pulling them in turn
until Natasha gasped, writhing in anticipation.

'I want you,' she cried, moving to rain kisses all over
his body.

Tearing the last separating articles of clothing from
themselves, she swung her leg over his body and
lowered herself on to him. His hands grasped her to
him as they began their rhythmic movement. Slowly
at first, sensually, provocatively, they moved in uni-
son, gradually building up the tempo. Natasha rev-
elled in ecstasy, keeping apace with his mounting
heights, watching, waiting, wishing it would last for
ever, yet yearning for its pulsating finale.

At last, they reached it together and she gave in to
her desire, wave after wave of passion surging over
her, as Anton brought her to her exhilarating climax.

They lay still for a long time in each other's arms,
neither wanting to break the spell that had brought
them to such an unbelievable vortex of pleasure.
Natasha snuggled into the crook of his neck, a beautiful smile across her face, and feeling safe in his

strong embrace, slept.

She awoke with a shiver she did not know how long afterwards and Anton stirred beside her, reaching into a locker to produce a blanket which he spread over them. She raised her head and looked down at him.

'Was I good enough?'

'Good enough? Heavenly! I told you I could see the signs in you, didn't I? I can tell you, that surpassed everything.'

'Everything,' she agreed, kissing him lightly on the nose.

Their stomachs told them eventually it was time to move and Natasha ate the best meal of her life a few minutes later, from the lunch provided by Sally.

'Happy?' he asked, smiling affectionately across the repositioned table at her.

'Happy,' she returned, 'except for one thing.'

'What?'

She laughed at the doubtful expression on his face. "No, you fool. Nothing wrong with you. It's just...'

'Well?'

'It's just that it won't last.'

'Why shouldn't it? We both obviously need each other. What better reason for a lasting relationship?'

'You have to go tomorrow.'

'Oh, yes, you mean that. I know. But we have to accept that our careers will keep us apart sometimes. Just think of the moments we can be together. Our futures can be planned so as to ensure a minimum of separation.'

'I suppose so.'

'It'll work out OK, don't you worry.'

'Oh, this and that,' Natasha replied light-heartedly to Tom's question as to how they had spent their day.

'And the other,' Suzy added crudely. 'Admit it, you might as well.'

Natasha took her friend to one side.

'How do you know what we've been up to? And anyway, why should I tell you?'

'For a start, it's the look in your eyes, wild yet dreamy.'

Natasha blushed. 'Is it that obvious?'

'Definitely!'

'Well, draw your own conclusions, my dear. Apart from that, we had such a peaceful day.'

She described the route they had taken after lunch, all the birds they had seen, as well as glimpses of the mountainous region far to the north and east.

They had, in fact, travelled quite a distance in the small cruiser, content with each other's company. Sometimes they had talked, often standing arms round each other, frequently lost in passionate kisses. The future was always on the agenda.

'I have a week in Los Angeles,' Anton had told her, 'then a few days meeting business associates on my way home.'

'So you'll be home in a fortnight?'

'A long fortnight away from you.'

Natasha felt a warm glow at these words. He would miss her, almost as much as she would him.

'Two weeks will pass very quickly,' he persuaded her, 'then you'll be in my arms again.'

She had even contemplated suggesting that she could accompany him to Los Angeles, but thought better of it. Besides he would be working. No, it was best left as it was. She and Suzy had a flight booked

around the same time as Anton's return to the UK.
She would have to wait till then to see him again.

The moment of his departure came too soon, their
farewell swift and rather formal in view of the assem-
bled company. She stood on the jetty, watching until
the boat was a tiny speck nearing the mainland, then
it was lost in a mass of other craft near the far shore.
Tom returned an hour later with a few provisions
from the harbour.

He gave his sister a squeeze.

'Forgiven?'

'Entirely, my dear big brother. Your little trick
turned up trumps.'

'We're so relieved,' added Sally standing at Tom's
side. 'I must confess I had misgivings. There's nothing
worse than people match-making or trying to organize your life for you. It could have been disastrous.'

'But it wasn't, thanks to you all.'

'He's sure smitten by you,' grinned Tom. 'He talked
of nothing else all the way to the shore.'

Natasha shut herself away in the bedroom for a
while, needing her own company, to sort out her
addled brain. Things had progressed so rapidly she
wanted to draw breath. How strange it still seemed
that she could love so deeply a man whom she had
hated at first meeting. How wonderful that he loved
her too.

But did he? When had he ever mentioned the word
'love'? He hadn't! He had said he wanted her, needed
her. He had shown his physical attraction towards
her in an amazingly satisfying fashion. He had talked
of the future when they could be together again.
Natasha felt sparks of desire rise in her in anticipation of that. But she had no evidence that he loved her.

Despite her attempts to blot him out, a vision of Pomfret materialized before her. She could hear those ugly words over and over. She knew them by heart. Old doubts flooded back.

Not for the first time she chastised herself vehemently. This solitary thinking was not good for her. It was parting from Anton that had put her in this frame of mind. Be positive, she ordered her negative self. Fill your time with so much activity that you won't have time to deliberate.

She joined the others, who now numbered just four, all the remaining guests having departed for the mainland.

'Right, Tom,' she announced. 'We're all yours. What's on the agenda for the rest of our stay?'

Much to their utter surprise and delight, Natasha and Suzy were rushed off their feet from that moment onwards. Sally had organized a flight to Calgary, from where they hired a four-berth camper van. Natasha had always had a secret wish to see the Rockies and she certainly was not disappointed by the breathtaking, immense beauty of the miles upon miles of rugged, snow-capped mountains.

They travelled in a north-westerly direction, putting in great distances each day along wide sweeping highways with Tom and Sally sharing the driving. It was a balmy evening when they at last approached the coast near Prince Rupert and embarked on a cruise ship which was to bring them all the way down the coast, back to Vancouver.

During the trip, Natasha had found every opportunity to search for and buy American national newspapers, which reported on Anton's progress.

'Tasha's passionately in love with him,' Sally confided in her husband one day. 'I just hope she won't get hurt this time.'

'You worry too much,' he assured her. 'Let things take their course. They were made for each other.'

Natasha carefully cut out all references to Anton that she could find, keeping them in an envelope. She would stick them in the scrapbook when she got home.

The ship was as grand as the camper had been basic, with fine cabins, lounge, dining-room and a large bar. Natasha's eyes lit up when she caught sight of a piano in the corner of the lounge. She had not played a note for almost three weeks and apart from being very bad discipline, she missed it. There was a tiny replica of a grand piano on the lid of the real one.

'My client would like to try out your piano,' Suzy boldly stated to the captain on the first morning after breakfast.

'Suzy!' Natasha felt embarrassed at her friend's boldness.

'She's an international pianist,' Suzy confided in a few interested passengers.

Before she could refuse Natasha found herself seated before the keys of what looked like a good quality piano. Its tone did not disappoint her, though it was in need of tuning. She began tentatively, nervous at the growing interest in her, but soon her love of playing took over and she worked through some of her repertoire.

'*New York Echo*,' a Southern-states drawl spoke beside her.

She finished the piece and turned to the redhead beside her.

'I beg your pardon?'

'I'm from the *New York Echo*,' she repeated. 'Actually I'm on holiday over here, but this would make a lovely story. Natasha Spitzen, isn't it?'

'How did you know?'

'It's my business to know. I heard them call you Tasha, and did some research.'

Natasha eyed her cautiously, not able to fully trust anyone of her profession after the rub with the tabloid press.

'Interesting name – is it your own, or your stage name?'

'My own.'

'Spitzen – is that German?'

'Swiss, actually.' Natasha was beginning to feel her temper fraying. 'My father was Swiss.'

'Ah, and what are you doing here, may I ask?'

'Like you, I'm supposed to be on holiday, taking a rest before returning to England to quite a heavy schedule.'

'Thank you, Miss Spitzen. Our readers may well be interested in your story. Up and coming pianist – the human touch – you know what I mean.'

Natasha did not know what she meant, but had not the inclination to ask. She just hoped the 'story' would be simple and truthful, that was all.

She resumed her impromptu recital, which was well applauded, and led Suzy out on the deck. 'Next time you feel like acting *agent extraordinaire*, will you please consult me first?'

'Sorry, Tash, but if you'd seen the light in your eyes at the sight of a piano, you'd have done the same. I thought for a minute it was Anton you'd seen there in the corner, your expression was so keen.'

'Would that be Anton Martineau?' drawled the voice behind them. They both swung round on the

American.

'No, Anthony Taylor, actually,' interjected Suzy quickly. 'You wouldn't know him. He's a friend of ours in England.'

The reporter looked disappointed and left them alone.

'Brilliant, Suzy. Thanks.' Natasha hugged her friend. 'I was struck dumb. She was a bit near the mark!'

The ship travelled smoothly towards Vancouver, reminding Natasha of her ecstatic day on the boat and Anton. Her thoughts often turned to him and subconsciously she found herself playing parts of the Tchaikovsky concerto as part of her subsequent recitals. By popular request, she gave two performances each day until they docked in Vancouver, the captain presenting her with the tiny piano after her final piece was ended.

'Thank you,' she said with genuine enthusiasm. 'I fell in love with that on day one. I'll treasure it always.'

'What a story!' they heard the familiar voice say as they left the ship to return to Tom's flat for the last day of the holiday.

Too soon came the farewells, the thanks and the promises. Tom and Sally drove them to the airport.

'Take care,' called Sally as the two friends approached the gate.

'Hope all goes well with you know who,' shouted Tom.

Natasha blew her brother a kiss, her eyes full of tears.

'Well, I like that,' Suzy joked, seeing Natasha's difficulty. 'After all their promises, here I am going home without a man. I shan't come next time.'

Their flight took off without delay, both women silent, taking a last look at the place where they had both enjoyed their most enjoyable holiday ever. Natasha slept fitfully as the plane covered the vast distance across the entire continent. She was suddenly wide awake as she felt the plane begin its descent into JFK airport. It was a scheduled stop for refuelling and she hoped they would be airborne again immediately. It was not to be.

'Ladies and gentlemen, we apologize, but we have a small technical hitch. We have to ask you to leave the aircraft for a short while.'

They were ushered through the dark wet night into a large lounge area for what turned out to be a three-hour wait. Natasha bought some newspapers in case there were any late reports of Anton's progress. Forgetting her experiences on the cruise, she bought a copy of the *New York Echo* and turned to the music pages.

What caught her eye made her reel with shock. Her own face stared back at her from the printed page. She closed the paper in horror.

'What's up?'

She handed the paper to Suzy, who opened it at the correct page. She studied the picture, comparing it with the pale face opposite her.

'A good likeness,' she teased, beginning to read. As she read her eyes grew wider and wider.

'What does it say?' Natasha demanded.

'First it tells the truth, of our holiday, your chance meeting with her, your piano recitals.'

'Go on.'

'I'll get to the ridiculous bit – "Her eyes misted over

as she played a romantic melody that reminded her of the one she loves ... the boy next door left behind in England ... her self-confessed lover Anthony Taylor". My God! They do make a meal out of people, don't they?'

Natasha stared at the article in disbelief and anger at being misrepresented. Some of these so-called journalists certainly had a lot to answer for at times. She just hoped that no one important to her would see the offending article.

She succeeded in shutting further such thoughts from her mind as they were called for the resumption of their flight. Now Heathrow was only seven hours away she simply could not wait to be home, to feel the old familiar comfort of her flat again after over three weeks away.

Suzy was unusually quiet, too, and both of them watched the in-flight film to occupy the long boring hours.

I wonder if he's home yet? Natasha mused as the plane began the gradual descent. She swallowed hard as her ears popped uncomfortably. She hated this bit even more than take-off and was always relieved when she felt the wheels touch down on the tarmac.

They slipped through Customs relatively swiftly as they were British passport holders and were going through the green channel, but Natasha could not believe how exhausted she felt as they hailed the taxi outside the terminal.

'I don't suppose he'll phone tonight,' she almost shouted to Suzy over the volume of the cab driver's radio. 'He may not be home yet.'

Suzy shook her head.

'He wasn't sure, was he?'

'Maybe I'll hear tomorrow.'

She closed her eyes, a blissful smile across her lips. To be held in those arms again was all she desired for the moment, reassurance that he cared and that he wanted her again.

The flat seemed cold and unwelcoming and Natasha felt deflated, somewhat depressed.

It must be the jet lag, she persuaded herself, switching on the fire despite the spring air. She made herself a mug of strong black coffee. She had no wish to sleep yet or her personal clock would be completely haywire, but she lay on her stomach on the rug while she waited for the coffee to be cool enough to drink. She surveyed the room, acknowledging each item like an old friend. Her eyes came to rest finally on her piano, its lid closed, a film of dust on its mahogany sheen. Getting up, she hurriedly finished the coffee and went to open the piano.

'Maybe he'll phone tomorrow,' she reminded herself as she began to play.

The telephone failed to ring once the next day, but although Natasha could not help her disappointment, she pushed it to the back of her mind.

'He's obviously not back yet,' she said out loud as she embarked on another intensive day of practising. Despite rather a persistent ache that she blamed again on her long flight, she knew she must return to her disciplined schedule of practice. She had a heavy programme of recordings and concerts during the rest of the spring and throughout the summer. In fact she was expecting Suzy round the next day to synchronize dates and other arrangements.

She had a lesson booked with Norman Flaxman in a few days, too, and she needed to impress him. She would never be able to admit to him that she had spent such a long period of time without playing a single note. He would be horrified!

Suzy arrived early for their agreed appointment.

'Still no call,' sighed Natasha as she let her agent in. 'I can't imagine that he's still in the States, can you?'

'I suppose not,' shrugged Suzy avoiding meeting Natasha's eye. 'It's early days yet. Be patient.'

Patience was not what Natasha was experiencing at that moment, anything but. This waiting for a promised call for the third day in succession was preying on her nerves. She felt irritable and snapped several times as the morning progressed.

By the time Suzy left they were both more than a little annoyed with each other and had begun saying things that they normally would not have said.

'I'd better go. We'll continue this when you're in a less foul mood.'

'Me? I like your cheek.'

'Admit it, Tash, you're unbearable today.'

'It'll make all the difference when he phones.'

'*If* he phones more like.'

'What do you mean by that?' Natasha shouted, but Suzy had gone, slamming the door behind her.

Eight

Natasha brooded on Suzy's words all that day. What had she meant – "*if* he phones"? Did Suzy know something she didn't? Or was she just being Devil's Advocate?

Natasha resisted the temptation to phone her agent for fear of being misunderstood. Suzy might take the call as an attempt to apologize, but apologize she would not!

She disciplined herself enough to practise some more before her lesson, however, and made a conscious effort to appear well-prepared and calm.

I am a professional, she kept reminding herself. I can't afford to let my emotions come between me and my career. I've already lost one tutor through over-hasty reaction. I can't afford to lose another.

By the end of the week, her efforts to hide her disappointment were wearing very thin. To tell the truth she was beginning to feel a fool. Everyone she knew well enough to be aware of her attachment to Anton had asked her how her romance was progressing. Suzy had phoned partly to clear the air between them, Natasha realized, but mainly to satisfy her curiosity on news of Anton. Norman, who had suspected the mutual attraction between the two musicians, asked if she had seen the maestro lately.

Tom phoned twice from Vancouver. The first time he was in provocative mood, teasing his sister about

127

her affair, joking about his part in bringing them
together. The second time he was much more cau-
tious, talking about general matters relating to his
own life, Suzy, her musical commitments. It was only
after every other subject had been broached that he
tentatively asked, 'Has he phoned you yet?'

'Oh, Tom, no, not yet. I begin to think he won't
phone at all. He must be in the UK by now. In fact, I
happen to know he has a series of concerts with the
Philharmonia in a couple of weeks. He'll need to be
back for rehearsals.'

'Is there any way you can find out if he's back?'

'Not without drawing attention to myself, but I
might ask Suzy to do a bit of probing for me.'

'Good idea, Sis. Now don't you fret. There's got to be
an excellent explanation for his silence. You wait and
see.'

'I hope you're right.'

Suzy's investigations proved more heart-rending
than Natasha had dreaded.

'He's been back for ten days, I'm afraid, mainly
spent in the recording studios, from what I can make
out,' admitted Suzy, with whom Natasha had regained her former closeness. She gave her client a
hug. 'Don't worry,' she went on. 'He's been rushed off
his feet. Besides, he probably thinks we're still over in
Canada. I expect he's forgotten when we were due
home.'

Natasha was not convinced by her friend's attempts
at persuasion. He couldn't be that absent-minded to
have forgotten. He couldn't be so busy that he didn't
have time to phone her. No. Something was wrong,
somewhere.

That night in bed Natasha's confused mind retraced the events of the past few weeks. She tried to add up everything that had been said, unable to believe that a man could behave towards her as he had done without some genuine feeling on his part. Unless....

She pushed those memories to the back of her brain. She refused to accept Pomfret's words. She could not, would not believe those accusations.

Then another thought crossed her mind as she remembered the reporter on the cruise and the subsequent article in the *New York Echo*. Could Anton have read that pack of lies? Did he seriously think she had an on-going relationship with 'the boy next door', as the writer had put it? Surely not.

But what could she do? She hated the prospect of continuing in this fashion, not knowing. Should she phone him? That thought had occurred to her before, but she had always rejected it. He would think she was too presumptuous.

Eventually, after promising herself that she would give him two more days before contacting him, she fell into a deep sleep. She dreamed a strange disturbing dream which she could not understand and woke in the morning with a headache.

There was one other matter preying on her mind. It was there in black and white for her to see, in her diary. In less than a month she had an engagement in the Festival Hall to play the Tchaikovsky Piano Concerto again, under the baton of one Anton Martineau. She had been looking forward to that event since their time together in Vancouver, but as the days dragged on with no sign of him attempting to phone her, the prospect began to fill her with foreboding.

'But that's ages yet,' Suzy tried to console her. 'Everything will be OK by then.'

Two agonizing days passed. Thankfully for Natasha, she had much to occupy her. She was rehearsing for a concert that week in Liverpool.

'He'll try to contact me while I'm away,' she told herself as the train sped north. 'That can be my excuse to phone him, to apologize for missing his call!'

In the soloist's room in the concert hall she found a single red rose. Her heart lifted. Just like the one in her hotel room in Berlin. From him? She would allow herself to believe so until denied, but she would not be the one to bring the subject up.

She gave what she described over the phone to Suzy later as a mediocre performance that evening. There was nothing wrong with it, she had to admit, but nothing quite right either. The conductor was very correct, demanding a high level of discipline from the orchestra and soloist, but he failed to inspire anyone into the realms of the extraordinary.

'Not like Anton,' she could not help confiding in Suzy. 'He certainly had the knack.'

'Talking of Anton, by the way.'

'Yes?' Natasha felt her pulse quicken in anticipation. 'Have you heard from him?' she found herself asking.

'Not exactly, but another of my clients had the honour of meeting him after a concert.'

'Well?'

'He was rude, pig-headed, in fact the most obnoxious man she had ever laid eyes on – her very words, I'm afraid.'

Natasha did not know whether to laugh or cry, but bit her lip hard and remained silent.

'Are you still there?'

'Yes.'

'Sorry, Tash. I didn't mean to upset you. I only told you because I thought it sounds as if he's missing you.'

'Or feeling guilty, more like. Was he alone?'

'Ellen didn't say.'

'She hasn't fallen for him, has she? You remember that was exactly my first impression. I've seen him behave like that, towards me. I can't understand him. I really can't.'

'When do you expect to be home?'

'The first train I can catch in the morning. I'll ring you later on from the flat.'

The more Natasha deliberated on Suzy's words, the more her decision to phone him strengthened. She would call him the minute she reached home, she hoped by midday. She would ask him straight out why he had failed to phone. She would enquire as to his feelings for her, demand point blank if there was another woman in his life.

By the time she reached home, however, this resolve had worn away, leaving a nervous, timid young woman, afraid to pick up the phone. The journey had been long and tedious, with delays and unscheduled stops. It was already nearly four o'clock. She poured herself a generous measure of whisky and calmed herself by unpacking her case slowly and methodically. Swallowing the last of her drink, she picked up the phone and dialled his number.

She lost count of how many times she heard it ring at his end, before she slammed down the receiver, frustrated. She felt cheated. She had not planned for that. Having psyched herself up to make the call she had assumed he would have the decency to answer. Now what?

She consulted the list she had compiled of his

commitments. There was nothing mentioned for this afternoon. So where was he? Who was he with?

And so on and so on, she chided herself angrily. Why does your suspicious mind always have to draw the same conclusions? Trust him. There's bound to be a quite legitimate explanation for everything.

Not able to face speaking to Suzy at that juncture, she left the phone off the hook until its high-pitched squeal forced her to replace it.

She sighed. She might as well try again.

'Hello?'

Natasha almost dropped the telephone.

'Anton?' she whispered.

'Who is it?'

'It's me.'

'Tasha, is that you?'

'Yes.'

'Where have you been? I've been trying to get you.'

'Liverpool,' she said attempting to hide the disappointment. The red rose could not have been from him, after all. 'But I've been back from Canada for ages.'

'Good holiday in the Rockies?'

'Wonderful, thanks. And a super trip in a boat from Prince Rupert all the way down the coast. It's all beautiful.'

'Mmm.'

He sounded so cool in comparison to her surging emotions. What had she done to deserve this? Her thoughts returned to the American reporter on the ship and the newspaper article that resulted from their chance meeting. Could that really be the cause of his sang-froid?

'I missed you,' she said, hoping it did not sound like

a whine. 'I thought of you often.'

She wanted so much for him to say he had missed her too and thought of her often, but he did not respond.

'When can we meet?' she went on. 'I'm free tomorrow morning.'

'I'm busy tomorrow, rehearsing all day.'

'What about the next day?' She consulted her diary. 'Oh, no. I can't make it then.'

If she had not been almost as busy as him she would have believed he was putting off their meeting for ever. Finally, they agreed on a mutually free date five days hence and he promised to call for her at eight.

The next few days seemed like an eternity to Natasha despite two recording sessions, several rehearsals and a concert during that time. She had to agree with the newspaper music critic that her concert performance gave the impression that her heart was not quite in it. It wasn't! This man would be the ruin of her, careerwise, if she did not look out. Suzy told her as much the next day in no uncertain terms.

'Look here, Tasha.' She stood hands on hips, a severe expression on her face. 'I stand to make a fortune out of you if I play my cards and you play your notes right!'

'Point taken, boss.' She laughed, then more seriously, 'You're right, of course. I must buck my ideas up.'

'When are you seeing Anton?'

'Tonight.'

'Then tell him from me to stop messing about or I'll give him something to think about.'

'I'll tell him,' promised Natasha, intending no such thing.

The customary pre-meeting nerves dominated her afternoon. They had agreed to return to the pub in Epping Forest as they were quite anonymous there besides its being a welcoming place to spend an evening. She hoped the atmosphere between them would be as warm, too. Well, it would not be long before she found out.

He looked as handsome as ever as his muscular form stood framed in the doorway on the dot of eight o'clock. She smiled up shyly at him, melting in his gaze. He kissed her lightly on the lips, more as a matter of politeness than passion, she realized with regret.

'Sorry I haven't been in touch with you before,' he said over his shoulder as he led the way to the car. 'Apart from being unbelievably busy, I've got a few problems I've been trying to sort out.'

Problems? Her heart froze with dread. What was he going to say next?

He said nothing more until they were well out of the metropolis. He drove fast, but Natasha had every confidence in his skill, the car snaking its way into the countryside.

'I've been down to Devon.'

His words came out of the blue, making Natasha jump. She remembered the time they had met there by chance.

'Family problems,' he went on.

'Nobody ill, I hope?'

She was beginning to feel a little better. If it was only family problems he had to deal with, it posed no threat to her. She sighed, sinking deeper into the soft seat beside him.

'No, nothing like that. A disagreement, I'm afraid.

One that causes me much distress.'

He swung the car into the gravel forecourt of the pub and they walked in silence into the oak-beamed bar. Anton had to stoop his head to reach the table, the same one as before, and it was some while before Natasha dared to speak.

'Would it help to talk about it?'

Anton was obviously preoccupied by the subject he had introduced. He shook his head vehemently.

'You wouldn't be able to help,' he answered tetchily.

'Sorry. I didn't mean to interfere in something that doesn't concern me.'

'I....'

He would say no more. Despite Natasha's curiosity being whetted and her several attempts at broaching the subject, he would not be drawn. Puzzled by this mystery, but determined not to let it ruin the entire evening, Natasha sought hard for a new topic of conversation. They discussed music, their full engagement diaries and various parts of the world that they had visited.

This is getting us nowhere, Natasha sighed to herself. It's as if we're absolute strangers, not lovers. Not once has he shown any warmth, or referred to Canada. What is the matter? Well, it will have to be me that makes all the running, I suppose.

She reached forward across the table and took his hand.

'I've missed you.'

She knew she had said that over the phone; she realized it sounded rather clichéd, but it was true.

'I've missed you, too,' he murmured so quietly Natasha almost missed what he said. His hand squeezed hers for a moment then his thumb began gently to stroke the back of her hand.

So he hasn't forgotten, she rejoiced, responding to his touch. He hasn't completely discarded me like a once-used plaything.

The eyes he raised to hers were warm, tinged with sadness.

'Shall we go?'

'So soon?'

'It's pleasant here, but impersonal. You can invite me in for coffee, if you like.'

A flicker of a smile flashed across his features for a moment as they left half finished drinks on the table and made for the door.

He's coming round, Natasha told herself, her hand nestling firmly in his. He has managed to dispel his troubles and relax.

She desperately wanted him to take her in his arms and kiss her hungrily, but she knew she must be patient. She must woo him carefully, to be certain of him. She must not push him too fast or she might lose him.

The silence in the car during their return was one of reconciliation rather than tension between them. Natasha was amazed how quickly they drew up at the apartments and she was unlocking her door. She dared not turn round to him, but made straight for the kitchen and put the kettle on. She heard him close the door and felt his presence behind her, leaning against his chest as his arms enfolded her. He rested his face on the top of her head until the kettle boiling disturbed them. He released her until she had made the coffee and carried it into the lounge and put it down on the table. Then he pulled her down on the sofa, enclosing her tenderly in his arms again.

'Your hair is so soft,' he whispered, nuzzling into the back of her neck. 'Oh, Tasha!'

It was almost a cry, that made her sit up and face him. The sadness in his eyes distressed her.

'What is it, my love?' She kissed his eyes one after the other, then his nose and tentatively, his lips.

'Tasha!' he repeated, this time with longing, his mouth taking hers with a ferocity that stunned her.

'I love you,' she gasped as he paused to kiss her chin, her neck, her breasts. 'I want you, Anton. Make love to me, please.'

She was in his arms, being transported across the lounge to her bedroom. She was laid gently on the bed, her eyes closed, revelling in the touch of his hands, excited by the masculine scent of him, aroused by the anticipation of his body.

'No!' The shout that erupted from his lips both startled and frightened her. She opened her eyes to see him buttoning his shirt as he turned from her.

'Anton? But why?'

'I'm sorry, Tasha, my love. I'm sorry!'

She was crying, shaking with the shock of his rejection.

'It's too complicated to explain. I've racked my brain for an explanation. I've blamed myself a million times for wanting you and even more for hurting you.'

He was making for the door. She held out her arms to him, hoping in vain that he would return.

'I promise you'll understand one day. I've tried to fight my growing love for you. But it's no good. I must go.'

Natasha was left sobbing bitterly into her pillow and that was where she stayed for the rest of the night, not bothering to get undressed, not sleeping until the dawn.

'I'm ill,' she groaned to Suzy the next morning. 'It must be the flu. You'll have to cancel the concert tomorrow night.'

'You sound as if you've been crying. Are you sure it's flu?'

'Of course I'm sure,' she snapped. 'I feel terrible.'

'OK. I'll cancel the concert, if you're certain you won't be fit. I'll be round later.'

'No, don't come round here. I don't want to see anyone. I mean I don't want to give anyone my germs,' she added hurriedly.

'Have it your way,' Suzy answered suspiciously, 'but I'll come tomorrow.'

Natasha did not reply. She felt sure she never wanted to see another living soul, ever again, but had no inclination to say it.

'Till tomorrow, then.'

Natasha stayed in her room for most of the day, eating and drinking nothing, crying every time her thoughts returned to the events of the previous evening.

Why, oh why? The question recurred over and over in her troubled mind. Ever since she had first met him, he had shown a reluctance on occasions, as if held back by something or someone unknown. He had said that before, one day you'll understand, but at this moment she was damned if she did.

It was becoming dark when she at last ventured into the lounge. She switched on the light, blinking against the glare, bursting into floods of tears at the two full coffee cups still where they had been abandoned the night before. She carried them shakily into the kitchen, emptying them down the sink.

'Symbolic!' she muttered. 'My love poured down the drain!'

She helped herself to a large glass of whisky before returning to the bedroom where she attempted to forget everything in sleep.

It was an extremely red-eyed, bad-tempered young woman who reluctantly let her agent into her apartment the following morning.

'Tash!' Suzy exclaimed at the sight. 'You poor dear.'

Natasha could not speak.

'So you know.'

'Know what?'

'I didn't want to be the one to break the bad news to you.'

'What bad news? Suzy, don't mess about.'

Gingerly, Suzy reached into her bag and produced a copy of *The Times*. She turned a few pages, keeping her eye on Natasha, who watched with a confused expression on her tear-stained face.

'Oh, hell!' Suzy spat out as she found the page, folding the paper small enough to hand to her friend. She had circled the appropriate paragraph in green ink, so Natasha's eyes were guided to the spot instantly.

Natasha's eyes widened as she read, then she threw down the newspaper and buried her head in her hands with a cry of despair.

'Oh, no!'

'I thought you must have heard already?'

Natasha vehemently shook her head, her hair falling as a dark curtain in front of her face.

'It can't be true. Please tell me it's a mistake,' she moaned, turning away.

'I truly am sorry, Tash. You must hurt like hell.'

In answer, Natasha reached to read the paragraph once again before ripping the page into tiny pieces. But what she had read stood out vividly before her, imprinted on her mind for ever.

FORTHCOMING MARRIAGES

The Honourable Sir Humphrey and Lady Fiona Pinkerton-Smythe of Buckfast Abbey have the greatest pleasure in announcing the betrothal of their only daughter, Maria, to Anton Martineau of Devon.

Nine

'That's it! I'm finished!'

'What do you mean, finished? With what?'

'With men, with my career, with....'

'Now just you hang on a minute, Tasha. Don't you go making such devastating and final remarks. I've always advised you not to take the opposite sex seriously. I don't and I've never been hurt yet.'

'So you don't understand how I feel. You've got no right to lecture me.'

'I'm not doing any such thing, you goose. I'm just trying to get you to see your position in perspective. And as for your career, it's criminal to even suggest an end to that.'

'But I just can't face going on.'

'Look. The other day I joked with you about my wanting to become rich as your agent. Well, I'm not denying that, but honestly, Tasha, you're brilliant. The world is your oyster. You have reached the stage when I can begin to be choosy now. I can actually refuse engagements. Everyone wants to hear you play. You can't even begin to think of throwing that away, you really can't.'

'But I love him.'

For several minutes Suzy was lost for words. There was no logical answer to that cry from the heart. She put her arm round Natasha's shoulder.

'There, there. I won't say any more today. I'll make

you some soup, then I'll go home and fetch my things. I'm spending a few days here with you.'

'But....'

'No buts. I'm adamant.'

She disappeared into the kitchen, leaving Natasha to mope for a while alone. She tried to rationalize the situation. At least she now understood what Anton had tried to tell her on several occasions. But why, if he was about to become engaged to Maria, had he encouraged her? Why did he take her out, kiss her, join the party in Canada? And finally, why had he made love to her so passionately? Why had he shown such an unfettered sexuality if he truly belonged to another?

Suzy returned with the soup.

'Drink it all up. I can't have you wasting away, can I?'

It certainly was delicious and Natasha felt slightly better after she had finished it. Suzy switched on the stereo, choosing a Mozart tape.

'Soothing music to calm you,' she said, kindly. 'Now you just lie here on the sofa while I dash home for my stuff. Don't move. I won't be long.'

She had only been gone a short while when the phone rang.

'Hello?'

'Tasha.'

She slammed down the receiver, staring at it as if she had seen a ghost.

How could he? How dare he? What did he want to do? Rub salt into the wound?

The phone rang again. She let it ring for a long time before finally giving in.

'Let me explain....'

Angrily, she almost threw the telephone across the room. Bloody nerve of the man! As if he hadn't done enough harm. If he tries again....

The bell of the telephone rang as if in answer to her threat.

I won't fall for it this time. Ring as long as you like, I won't pick you up. She stared defiantly at the offending machine, but it refused to stop. Eventually, she lunged at it and shouted into the mouthpiece.

'Leave me alone. Can't you see you've done enough damage?'

'Natasha, are you all right?'

'Norman, I'm sorry.'

'What's the matter? You sound in a bad way.'

'I've just had a nasty phone call, that's all.'

'You poor thing. Tell the police.'

'No, Norman. I'm all right really.' It was a lie. She was shaking all over. 'About my lesson?' she heard herself saying. 'Oh, yes, no problem. I'll be there as usual tomorrow.'

Suzy found her playing Mozart half an hour later.

'Soothing music, you said,' she smiled a watery smile. 'It's wonderful to play, too.'

Suzy did not interrupt Natasha's playing, relieved to see a little of her sanity returned. She felt her nerves calmed by the music. Thank goodness Natasha had seen sense.

'Anton phoned while you were gone.'

Natasha felt pleased that she could mention him by name without hysterics. Suzy looked startled.

'What did he say?'

'Not much. I didn't give him a chance. Something like, "let me explain". What do you think his game is, Suzy?'

'Goodness knows, but what did you say to him?'
'I slammed the phone down.'
'Good girl.'
Natasha recalled the third phone call.
'Thankfully, I said nothing obscene. I was sorely tempted, I can assure you.'

The next few days were almost impossible for Natasha. Every little thing seemed to remind her of Anton and although she went through the motions of practising for her next concert, her heart still refused to be in her playing. Suzy was as good as her word and stayed close by her friend's side for most of her waking hours. She guarded the telephone, only allowing those she deemed necessary to be passed on to Natasha.

Anton tried to speak with Natasha on many occasions, but his persistence was no rewarded.

'Sorry, you must have the wro number,' Suzy repeated each time and Natasha knew it was him.

'Why do you think he keeps phoning?' she asked.

'I don't know and I'm not going to find out. And nor are you,' she added noticing the wistful look in Natasha's dark eyes. 'The critics will be stunned by your performance both on the concert platform and in the studios.'

'Yes, boss.'

The pain was beginning to dull, thanks to Suzy's care and attention, but she could not forbid her thoughts to stray night and day to him. She closed her eyes, only to see his deep blue eyes penetrating her defences. Her sleep was disturbed by images of him, by sensations that she was held in his arms.

The first public performance she gave after the shock announcement was a successful one, a recital in the Wigmore Hall on London's South Bank. The audience received her well and the reviews in the following day's papers were unanimous in their approval. She automatically cut them out and stuck them into her scrapbook, though the activity had less and less meaning for her now.

'I do believe you are on the road to recovery,' beamed Suzy, congratulating Natasha, as well as herself.

Natasha nodded, unconvinced.

'Suzy,' she began, 'I know you're pleased with the way I've pulled myself together. So am I, for that matter.'

'Yes?'

'I have a problem on the horizon.'

'What?' Suzy knew perfectly well what Natasha was about to say.

'The Tchaikovsky. It's only two and a half weeks until I'm due to play it.'

'That's plenty of time,' answered Suzy too brightly.

'There's no way I can go through with it.'

'Come on, Tash. You can do it. You must, to prove to him that you don't care a fig for him.'

'But I do.'

'But you mustn't let him know that.'

'I can't face speaking to him, let alone performing such a piece with him in front of a capacity audience. I shall have to cancel.'

'No, Tash. At least not yet. Practise it in the meanwhile, then I'll ask you how you feel a week from now.'

Taking her friend's advice, Natasha began her systematic practice of the tricky concerto that had first brought her to the notice of the maestro himself. After all, she tried to convince herself, you proved yourself last time. You even scored against him in showing how masterfully you could play. But, try as she might, she would not be persuaded that she could attempt to go through with it. Every note contained a memory, each phrase reminded her of the harmony they had created together.

Suzy had returned to her own flat after less than a week of nurturing Natasha back to sanity. She seemed convinced of her success and had every confidence that the worst was over. Anton had stopped trying to contact Natasha. It was for the best, Suzy had said.

So Natasha was taken by surprise one morning when her practising was broken by the harsh sound of the telephone. Absent-mindedly she lifted the receiver.

'Hello?'

'So you've got rid of your guardian angel?'

'Anton?'

'Don't hang up on me, please, Tasha.'

'I don't see why I shouldn't. I haven't got anything to say to you.'

'But I've got so much to say to you.'

'I'm listening. You'd better make it sound convincing.' She was forcing herself to sound hard and uncaring, but her hand shook with emotion.

'I'm in the phone box on the corner. I'm coming up.'

Before Natasha could protest he had gone. She paced the floor, angry with herself for even talking to him. There was a light tap on the door. Should she ignore it? He would have to go away eventually.

The second knock was firmer, more persistent, wearing away her resolve.

'Tasha.'

It was always the way he said her name, she remembered, so gently, so persuasively. She could resist no longer, almost running to open the door.

'You'd better come in.'

She stepped back to avoid any physical contact between them, although his mere presence had instantly inflamed her senses.

You're making a big mistake, her inner self told her as she led him into the lounge, careful to sit on a chair, not risking an encounter on the sofa.

'You've come to discuss the Tchaikovsky?' she asked hurriedly. 'I'm not sure that I can go through with it, though I can still play it. Even a mere slip of a girl like me.'

'I haven't come here for that, Tasha, and you know it.' He had not reacted to her jibe.

'So what brings you to this part of town?'

'Don't you know?'

'No I don't. You've got a damned cheek coming here as if nothing had happened. I suppose you don't know what effect your behaviour has had on me? Or perhaps you do. Maybe it boosts your already inflated ego to hit a woman when she's down.'

Natasha's colour had risen, her eyes flaming with indignation.

'Shut up and listen, Miss Spitfire.'

'Listen to you, Mr Marvellous? I've listened to you before, and look where it left me.'

He stood up and strode across the small room towards her. Bending down he grasped both her wrists in his powerful hands, pulling her roughly upright before him. She wrenched her hands from his vice-like grip. They stared angrily into one another's eyes, neither flinching, both refusing to give in.

'It's all been a terrible mistake,' he began, speaking very quietly, his voice shaking with emotion.

'You're telling me!' Natasha forced a harshness into her normally gentle tones.

'Don't get me wrong. I'm deadly serious. It really has been a terrible mistake,' he repeated earnestly.

Natasha's heart lurched uncomfortably. What was he trying to say? She remained silent, holding her breath, waiting for him to clarify his statement.

'Can we sit down? I feel so formal standing here.'

Like an automaton, Natasha lowered herself beside him on the sofa without taking her eyes off his face. She was aware of the rapid beating of her heart, the colour high in her cheeks.

'Maria,' he said, pausing for a while as if unable to decide how to proceed, 'is a beautiful woman.'

Natasha bit her lip, unable to reply.

'She and I have known each other since we were tiny children. We almost grew up together, even had the same nanny for a while. Our families have been entwined one way or another for generations.'

Natasha listened patiently, her calm exterior belying the turmoil inside. Get to the point, her mind pleaded.

'As you know I am very close to my grandmother. She is an extremely dominant woman and usually has her way in everything. It has always been her wish that our families be united in a marriage.'

Natasha suddenly wanted to block her ears. She could not face what he was about to explain. A pallor had gradually replaced the flushed face. She swallowed hard.

'Since our early teens, Grandmother has reached the conclusion that that marriage she was craving would be between Maria and me. She has pushed us together in every circumstance possible and has regarded us as unofficially engaged for years.'

Natasha wished she could curl up and die, rather than have to hear any more.

'When I arrived home from Los Angeles, after our time together in Vancouver, I was summoned to Devon. Maria was there, too.

'It's time you two were married,' Grandmother stated. 'The advertisement will appear in *The Times* in the morning.'

'She would hear no arguments or remonstrations from either of us. Lo and behold, she was true to her word and the forthcoming marriage was fact. I've been through hell since then.'

'You've been through hell? And I suppose you think I haven't?' Natasha broke her silence, tears of anger mixing with those of despair. 'I wish you every happiness!'

Anton's arm enveloped her, but she shied away.

'Don't you try soft soaping me. I can't understand how you could be so cruel as to tell me all this. You'd better go. I never want to see you again.'

'But I haven't finished.' He replaced his arm round her slim shoulders, more firmly this time. She felt too weak to attempt to remove it.

'I've been back down to Devon on several occasions since then.'

'I bet you have,' retorted Natasha bitterly, 'to see her.'

'If by her you mean Maria, you'd be wrong.'

'But you love her.'

'I didn't say that.'

'But you're going to marry her.'

'I didn't say that, either.'

Natasha stared open mouthed at the handsome man so close to her. Did she hear correctly? And what was the meaning of that smile beginning to creep into the corners of his eyes.

'When I returned to Devon, it was to visit Grandmother. She is old and infirm, and I had to be careful and clever in my defiance of her. Eventually, on my last visit which was yesterday, I managed to convince her.'

'Of what?'

'That I love another. She took it calmly in the circumstances, especially when she learned that Maria is similarly attached to someone else.'

Natasha's head swam as she became aware of the gentle hand caressing her hair as it fell across her shoulders. The smile had gone from his eyes, but their deep blue had become hypnotic.

'Tasha?'

She gazed at him in disbelief, her body tingling with electric charges. The impossible, the dream that had recurred so often, seemed to be coming true.

'You say that you love another?' she dared to whisper. 'Who is the lucky lady?'

He cupped his hand under her chin and drew her to him.

'It's you I love,' he said as their lips met lightly. 'I tried not to love you, but I fell for that raven-haired spitfire at our first meeting.'

The second kiss, long and arousing, told her all. It was true, she reminded herself over and over. He loves me!

'I thought....'

'I know what you thought, darling Tasha. I realize I should have come straight over here to you. My grandmother has an incredible power over me. I've tried to tell you several times, but made an entire mess of it.'

Natasha sighed a shuddering sigh, releasing the tension that had built up in her body over the past few weeks.

'Will you forgive me, Tasha?'

'On one condition.'

'Anything. What is it?'

She whispered in his ear, causing a broad smile to spread across his handsome features.

'You wicked creature! Your wish is my command!'

Hungrily, their lips met, Natasha responding to his penetrating tongue. Her hands explored his body, equalling his arousing manipulation of her, each undressing the other, until, scantily clad, Anton swept her into his arms and carried her through to the bedroom.

For a long time they excited and teased, Natasha provoking an urgent desire in him, Anton bringing her to the edge of fulfilment so many times. She wanted their love-making to last for ever, feeling all inhibitions melt away as his tongue left none of her body untouched.

Finally, when neither could delay their satisfaction a moment longer, she remembered the day on the boat as she drifted beyond the sensual thrill she had experienced then into a new dimension of erotic pleasure.

They lay exhausted and breathless, exultant in the heights they had reached together. No words were necessary.

'I forgot to tell you,' he confessed sleepily after many minutes' silence. 'There's to be an announcement in *The Times* tomorrow, denying the engagement of Maria and me.'

Natasha smiled happily, kissing him gently. Then she slept, cradled in the crook of his arm, contentment written on her face.

When Suzy let herself into the flat an hour later, she was puzzled by the various articles of clothing that lay strewn about the lounge. Her eyes took in the scene and it was not long before she realized that some obviously belonged to a male. She stood contemplating the bedroom door, frowning. Either Natasha had been attacked and raped by an intruder, or she had thrown herself into the arms of the first man who came along to compensate for losing Anton, or....

Surely not! A grin spread across her face as she walked to the door and slipped from the flat. She would give them an hour before phoning.

Natasha woke with a start at the sound of the telephone ringing in the other room. She kissed Anton's chin before carefully extricating herself from his arms, slipping her robe round her shoulders before leaving the bedroom.

'Hello?" she said, trying to bring herself back to reality.

'Now perhaps you'll return to your brilliant form, you nymphomaniac!'

'Suzy, I don't know what you mean.' She could not disguise the joy in her voice.

'I presume it is someone I know?'

'Suzy! I won't deny Anton is here, but...?'

Natasha could not help but blush when she heard that Suzy had actually been in the flat.

'Don't worry. I didn't linger. I got out like a shot when I twigged! But...?'

'We'll explain everything when we see you. Come round in an hour.'

Anton's body was warm as his arms welcomed Natasha's return. She discovered and responded to his arousal and they made love again, more gently this time, but equally satisfying none-the-less.

'Tasha, darling?'

'Mmm?'

'Would you agree if I put a third notice in *The Times*, to appear the day after tomorrow?'

'It depends what it says.'

'To announce our engagement, of course.'

'But you haven't asked me yet.'

'We can soon rectify that!' He paused, then, 'Miss Spitzen?'

'Yes, Mr Martineau?'

'Will you please do me the honour of becoming my wife?'

'With all my heart.'

The announcement of the engagement between these two shining stars of the music world caught the imagination of the press, who did their best to deny them a single minute's peace over the following few days. Tom phoned offering good luck with the concerto and repeated congratulations. Natasha had telephoned him as soon as she had accepted Anton's proposal.

There were many cards and letters from well-wishers, notably one from Anton's grandmother in Devon, summoning them to meet the old lady in three days' time. The fact that the next scheduled work for both of them was the Tchaikovsky concert provoked more than the usual rush of ticket sales and soon it became evident that they would be playing to a capacity crowd.

Natasha's raven hair shone with a beautiful lustre as she stood with Anton in the wings, waiting for their cue. Her dark evergreen satin evening gown complemented her high complexion and accentuated her slim shapely figure.

'You look gorgeous,' he murmured in her ear.

She smiled up at him, admiring the way the dark jacket contrasted with the deep golden hair.

Then, mutual attraction accepted, the welcoming applause of the audience drew them on to the stage. Natasha bowed in response to the enthusiasm that greeted her before settling herself at the piano. Glancing up to catch the eye of the man she adored, she indicated her readiness to begin.

The opening notes from the orchestra were her introduction and the adrenalin began to flow as the magic in her fingers once again captured Tchaikovsky's famous music. With absolute trust she remained aware of the maestro, following his mood and tempo, matching the rhythm of his body, piano and orchestra playing as one.

It was unanimously acclaimed the next morning in all the papers, but as Natasha cut them out to stick in her scrapbook later in the day, she chose one to be nearest to her own feelings.

'In their performance last evening of Tchaikovsky's Piano Concerto No. 1 in B-flat minor, Martineau and Spitzen complemented each other superbly, with mutual understanding and perfect harmony.

Miss Spitzen showed impetuosity and sparkle in the lively opening and final movements, con-

trasting with a deep, moving sensitivity in the slow movement.

Martineau produced a wonderful balance, drawing out the sensuality of Tchaikovsky's music. His mastery held soloist and orchestra together, bringing them simultaneously to an exotic climax. Their union is truly inspirational.

In this performance, Martineau and Spitzen uniquely portrayed this, one of Tchaikovsky's most famous compositions, in its true light, as a Passionate Concerto.